Shattered Crown

Michael Ferguson

Published by Michael Ferguson, 2024.

This is a work of fiction. Similarities to real people, places, or events are entirely coincidental.

SHATTERED CROWN

First edition. September 9, 2024.

ISBN: 979-8227472359

Written by Michael Ferguson.

Chapter 1: The Fall of the Holy Blade

Kade, a disgraced warrior-priest, sat alone in the shadow of the dying sun. The smoldering embers of a small fire crackled before him, the only sign of life in the barren wasteland that had become his home. Once, he had been known as the Holy Blade, a name whispered with reverence throughout the empire of Rethnor. Now, it was a curse, a reminder of the betrayal that had shattered not only his life but the entire realm.

His hand drifted instinctively to the jagged scar that ran across his chest, the mark left by the blade of his former brother-in-arms. He had survived the coup, the fall of the gods, and the collapse of the order he had sworn to protect, but at what cost? His mind tormented him with flashes of that fateful night, the screams of his fellow priests, the crumbling of the great temples, and the silence that followed. The gods, once the very foundation of Rethnor, had vanished, leaving nothing but despair in their wake.

Kade closed his eyes, but the memories refused to be banished. The weight of his exile hung heavy around him, and the guilt of his complicity gnawed at his soul. He had been part of the plot, however unwilling, to bring down the gods. He had believed in their fallibility, believed that mankind could rule itself without their guidance. He had been wrong.

A rustle of movement nearby snapped him out of his reverie. His hand instinctively went to the hilt of the sword at his side, though he hadn't drawn it in weeks. The wasteland was a desolate place, but not without its dangers. Bandits, scavengers, and worse roamed the land, preying on the weak and the broken. Kade was neither, but he no longer sought confrontation.

From the shadows, a figure emerged, cloaked in darkness, the hood obscuring their face. Kade's grip on his sword tightened, but he didn't draw it.

"Who are you?" he demanded, his voice hoarse from disuse.

The figure remained silent, stepping closer until the firelight illuminated a face that was both familiar and unknown. The man's features were sharp, his eyes glinting with a cold intelligence that sent a shiver down Kade's spine.

"I have been searching for you, Kade," the stranger said, his voice low and measured. "You are not easy to find."

Kade didn't respond, his mind racing. He had no enemies left, no allies, either. He was a ghost, a relic of a world that no longer existed.

The stranger stepped forward, his hand outstretched, revealing a sealed scroll. "I bring a message. A chance for redemption."

Redemption. The word felt foreign to Kade. Redemption had always been beyond his reach. He had been too deeply entrenched in the fall of the gods, too complicit in their betrayal. But the mention of it stirred something deep within him, a flicker of hope that he hadn't felt in years.

"I don't need your messages," Kade said gruffly, turning his back to the stranger. "I'm finished with this world."

The stranger didn't move. "You were once the Holy Blade, a man of honor and purpose. The world has fallen into chaos, and the gods' silence has left a void that can only be filled by darkness. But there is one way to bring balance back to Rethnor—to restore what has been lost."

Kade glanced over his shoulder. "And what would that be?"

"The Crown of the Fallen," the stranger said. "It is said to hold the power to resurrect the gods."

Kade's heart skipped a beat. The Crown of the Fallen was a legend, a myth told by desperate priests in the final days of the gods' reign. It had never been proven to exist, but if it did...

The stranger seemed to sense Kade's hesitation. "It was stolen long ago, hidden away by those who feared its power. But I know where it is. And I know that you are the only one who can recover it."

"Why me?" Kade asked, his voice tinged with bitterness. "I'm no longer a warrior. I'm a failure, a traitor."

"Because you are the only one who knows the truth about the gods' fall," the stranger said, stepping closer. "You were there. You were part of it. And you know what is at stake."

Kade clenched his fists, the weight of his guilt pressing down on him once more. He had tried to forget, to bury the memories of that night deep within his soul, but they had never left him. The gods' fall had not been a simple coup. It had been something far more sinister, something that even Kade had not fully understood at the time.

"The Crown is the only way to stop what's coming," the stranger continued. "An ancient evil is stirring, one that was bound by the gods long ago. If it is released, the world will be consumed in darkness."

Kade turned to face the stranger fully, his eyes narrowing. "And what if I refuse?"

The stranger's lips curved into a thin smile. "You won't. You seek redemption, even if you won't admit it. This is your chance to make amends for what you've done."

Kade stared at the stranger for a long moment, his mind warring with itself. He had sworn never to pick up a sword again, never to fight for a cause he didn't believe in. But the mention of the ancient evil, the hint of a danger that could destroy the world, gnawed at him.

Finally, he reached out and took the scroll from the stranger's hand. The seal was unbroken, marked with the sigil of a forgotten order, one that Kade had thought lost to time.

"I'll hear what you have to say," he said quietly, his voice barely above a whisper. "But I make no promises."

The stranger nodded, his eyes gleaming with satisfaction. "That's all I ask."

As the stranger disappeared into the night, Kade sat down by the fire, the scroll heavy in his hand. He stared at it for a long moment before finally breaking the seal and unrolling the parchment.

The words written there were simple, but they chilled him to the bone.

Find the Crown of the Fallen, or all is lost.

Kade closed his eyes, the weight of the message settling over him like a shroud. He had been given a chance at redemption, but it came with a price. A price that he wasn't sure he was willing to pay.

But deep down, he knew that he couldn't walk away. Not this time.

The gods may have fallen, but the world still needed saving.

And he was the only one left who could do it.

Kade leaned back against the rough bark of a towering oak, the crackling firelight flickering across his scarred face. The forest around him, despite the cold night, remained eerily silent, as if even the creatures of the woods were wary of him and his companions. His eyes flicked between the strangers that had now become his allies—a ragtag group he barely trusted, yet knew he couldn't complete the journey without.

Mira sat across from him, her deep violet eyes gazing into the fire. She was a mystery to him, her flowing robe adorned with symbols that Kade only vaguely recognized from the ancient texts of the fallen gods. Her power was undeniable, though she carried it with a quiet grace. She hadn't spoken much since they met, but Kade sensed something in her—something deeper than the mage she appeared to be.

Next to her, Tyra, the young thief, fiddled with a dagger, her fingers deftly twisting and twirling the blade with practiced ease. She had the sharp, suspicious gaze of someone who had spent her life on the streets, learning to trust no one and nothing. But there was something in her eyes, too—a fear she hid beneath layers of bravado. Kade had noticed the way her eyes darted to the sky whenever they passed under open air, as if she expected something to fall from above at any moment.

Finally, there was Sorin, the brooding mercenary. His massive frame was cloaked in black leather, and the hulking greatsword strapped to his back looked as though it could cleave a man in two with ease. His eyes never left Kade—there was no mistaking the tension between them. Sorin had made it clear that he was here for one reason: gold. He had no love for Kade, no respect for the man who had once been the Holy Blade, and it was clear he would not hesitate to turn on the group if the promise of coin grew thin.

Kade shifted uncomfortably. They were misfits, every one of them, bound together only by necessity. But in this broken world, where gods had fallen and chaos reigned, necessity was enough. He would need them for what lay ahead—if they didn't kill each other first.

Mira's voice broke the silence. "So," she began, her tone calm but firm, "are we going to talk about it?"

Kade glanced up at her, his brow furrowing. "Talk about what?"

"About why we're all really here," she said, her eyes locking onto his. "This isn't just a quest for a crown. You're not telling us everything."

Sorin grunted in agreement, crossing his arms over his chest. "I've been wondering the same thing. What's a disgraced priest doing hunting down a relic of the gods?"

Kade's jaw tightened. He had expected this. It was only a matter of time before the questions started, but the truth was far more dangerous than he had let on.

"I've told you what you need to know," he said, his voice cold. "The Crown of the Fallen is the key to restoring balance to the world. With it, we can resurrect the gods and stop the chaos."

Tyra snorted, flicking her dagger into the dirt. "Right. And you think we're just going to follow you because of that?"

Kade met her gaze, his eyes hard. "You're here because you need me. And I need you. That's all there is to it."

The fire crackled as the tension thickened between them. Mira was the first to break the silence.

"You may think you can keep your secrets, Kade," she said softly, "but the truth always finds its way out. Especially when it involves the gods."

Kade didn't respond. He wasn't ready to reveal the full extent of his past—not yet. The burden of his guilt, the role he had played in the fall of the gods, weighed too heavily on him. He had to keep moving forward, keep the focus on the task at hand. The Crown was the only thing that mattered now.

He rose to his feet, brushing dirt from his cloak. "Get some rest," he ordered. "We leave at first light."

The others exchanged glances but said nothing. One by one, they lay down by the fire, Mira the last to settle into her bedroll, her eyes lingering on Kade as if she could see through the walls he had built around himself.

Kade moved away from the fire, finding a spot just outside the circle of light. He leaned against a tree, staring up at the stars, his mind racing. He couldn't shake the feeling that things were already beginning to spiral out of his control. The journey was just beginning, but the weight of the past bore down on him like a storm, threatening to drown him before he could even take the first step.

As he stared at the sky, he thought of the gods—once so powerful, now silent. His chest tightened with the memory of the day they had fallen, the moment everything had changed.

His betrayal had set it all in motion, and now he was forced to live with that burden, every moment a reminder of what he had done.

But there was no time for self-pity. He had a mission to complete, and nothing—not even the ghosts of his past—would stop him from seeing it through.

The sun rose early the next morning, casting long shadows through the trees as the group gathered their supplies. Kade remained distant, focused on the path ahead, while the others prepared in silence.

They traveled in uneasy companionship, making their way through the dense forest, the air growing colder as they moved deeper into the unknown. The path was treacherous, littered with roots and hidden pitfalls, but they pressed on, each step taking them closer to their goal.

As the day wore on, the group began to fragment, each member retreating into their own thoughts. Tyra moved silently at the front, her eyes scanning the terrain ahead, while Sorin followed close behind, his hand resting on the hilt of his sword. Mira stayed near Kade, her expression thoughtful, as if she was trying to piece together the puzzle that was their leader.

It wasn't until the sun dipped below the horizon that they finally stopped for the night, setting up camp in a small clearing. Kade sat apart from the others, his back to the fire as he studied the map laid out before him.

"We're close," he muttered to himself, tracing a line with his finger. The map was old, worn with age, but the markings were clear. The Silent Temple lay ahead—his first destination, the place where his path to redemption would begin.

But even as he plotted their course, doubt gnawed at him. The journey ahead would not be easy. He had already put these people in danger by bringing them into his quest, and it would only get worse. The enemies they would face, the trials they would endure—none of them were prepared for what was coming. None of them, except perhaps Mira, knew the true stakes involved.

A sudden movement caught his attention, and he looked up to see Tyra standing over him, her arms crossed. Her face was shadowed, but her eyes gleamed in the firelight.

"What is it?" Kade asked, already knowing the answer.

"You're lying to us," she said flatly. "About why we're really here."

Kade's eyes narrowed. "I told you—"

"I don't care what you told us," Tyra cut in, her voice low but sharp. "I see things, Kade. I've always been able to. And I know there's something you're not telling us."

Kade's heart skipped a beat. Tyra's gift was no secret—she had mentioned her visions before, though he had dismissed them as fanciful tales. But the look in her eyes now made him reconsider.

She knelt down next to him, lowering her voice. "I've seen the Crown in my dreams," she whispered. "But it's not what you think it is."

Kade stiffened, his breath catching in his throat. "What did you see?"

Tyra hesitated, glancing around to make sure the others weren't listening. "I saw... darkness. A great shadow, wrapped around the Crown like a serpent. It was... alive."

A chill ran down Kade's spine. Tyra's words echoed his own fears, the doubts that had plagued him since he first set out on this journey. The Crown was supposed to be a symbol of hope, a way to restore the gods and bring balance back to the world. But what if it wasn't? What if the Crown was something far more dangerous?

Before he could respond, Tyra stood up, her expression unreadable. "You don't have to tell us everything," she said quietly. "But whatever you're hiding... it's going to come out eventually."

With that, she turned and walked back to the fire, leaving Kade alone with his thoughts.

He stared down at the map, his mind racing. Tyra's vision had shaken him more than he cared to admit. He had always known there were risks involved in seeking the Crown, but now he was beginning to wonder if those risks were far greater than he had anticipated.

The Crown was not just a relic of the gods—it was something more, something ancient and powerful, and perhaps... something evil.

Kade clenched his fists, his resolve hardening. Whatever the Crown's true nature, he had no choice but to find it. The fate of the world rested on his shoulders, and he would not allow it to fall into darkness.

Even if it meant sacrificing everything.

Chapter 2: Shadows of the Past

The journey to the Silent Temple was one marked by both anticipation and dread. Kade led the way through the rugged terrain, eyes sharp and focused despite the haze of guilt that had lingered for years. The air grew colder the closer they got to the temple's ruins, a chilling reminder of the gods' absence from the world.

Mira and Tyra walked a few paces behind him, their quiet conversations barely audible over the howling wind. Sorin, the mercenary, was further back, keeping watch on their rear as they ventured into increasingly dangerous territory. The road had long since disappeared beneath a thick carpet of overgrown brush and jagged rocks, forcing them to move slowly.

"Kade," Mira called out softly, breaking the long silence, "how much farther?"

"Not long now," he replied, his voice carrying a hollow echo of something lost long ago. "We'll reach the temple by nightfall, if we keep moving."

Tyra, the youngest of the group, seemed restless. Her sharp, bright eyes darted around the landscape, looking for threats that weren't there—or perhaps for something else. Ever since she'd mentioned seeing visions of the gods in her dreams, Kade had been watching her carefully. The gods had fallen, but there was something about her dreams that unnerved him, as if the gods weren't as distant as they seemed.

Mira, on the other hand, was harder to read. The mage carried herself with a practiced air of calm, yet Kade couldn't shake the feeling that she knew more about the prophecy than she let on. She hadn't been forthcoming with all the details of her own mission, and that secrecy weighed heavily on Kade's mind.

The temple was once a place of peace, a sanctuary for those who sought wisdom from the gods. But now, the very thought of returning to it filled Kade with dread. It was the place where his downfall had begun, where his betrayal had set events into motion that led to the gods' fall. He hadn't set foot there since that day, and the memories that lurked in those silent halls were ones he would rather forget.

Yet here he was, returning to the scene of his greatest failure, all because of the stolen Crown of the Fallen.

As they continued, the land around them began to change. The lush green grass gave way to dry, cracked soil, and the trees thinned out, their twisted branches reaching skyward like skeletal fingers. In the distance, Kade could see the jagged spires of the Silent Temple rising from the earth, casting long shadows in the fading light of the day. The temple had once been a majestic sight, its golden spires and white marble walls gleaming in the sunlight. Now, it was nothing more than a crumbling ruin, a tomb for the forgotten gods.

Tyra's footsteps slowed as they neared the temple. She glanced up at the towering ruins, her expression darkening. "It feels... wrong here," she said quietly, more to herself than to anyone else.

Kade nodded, but said nothing. He felt it too. The air was thick with something unseen, something malevolent. The gods had abandoned this place, but the echoes of their power—of their anger—still lingered. He could feel it in his bones.

"This is where you served?" Mira asked, her voice cutting through the tension. She studied the ruins, her gaze distant as though trying to piece together its past glory.

"Yes," Kade said tersely. "Before the fall."

Mira didn't pry further, though her eyes suggested she wanted to. Kade was grateful for her silence. He had no desire to recount the past, to relive the moments that had led to his exile.

The temple doors—massive slabs of stone engraved with ancient symbols—stood before them, partially ajar. Vines and moss had overtaken the once-ornate carvings, and the faint smell of decay wafted from within. Kade's hand instinctively went to the hilt of his sword, a force of habit from his years as a warrior-priest, though the weight of his blade felt more like a curse than a blessing these days.

"We'll camp inside," Kade said. "There's shelter in the inner sanctum."

"And what of the relic?" Sorin asked, finally breaking his silence as he caught up to the group. His eyes gleamed with the kind of hunger Kade had come to expect from men like him—men who lived for battle and bloodshed.

"The first clue to its location should be inside," Kade replied, though even he wasn't sure of that. The Silent Temple was rumored to hold many secrets, and Kade suspected that some of them were better left undiscovered.

They pushed through the heavy doors and stepped into the cold darkness of the temple's interior. The air inside was thick with dust, and the faint scent of long-extinguished incense clung to the stone walls. Faded murals adorned the walls, depicting scenes of the gods in their prime—wielding their divine powers, shaping the world, and guiding the people of Rethnor. But now, the murals were cracked and worn, the gods' faces obscured by time and neglect.

The group moved cautiously through the temple's halls, their footsteps echoing in the silence. Tyra kept close to Kade, her eyes wide as she stared at the remnants of the past. "I've seen this place before," she whispered.

Kade stopped in his tracks and turned to her. "What do you mean?"

Tyra hesitated, her gaze flitting from one mural to the next. "In my dreams... I've seen this place. The gods... they spoke to me here."

Mira glanced at Kade, her expression unreadable. "Could it be?"

Kade frowned. "The gods have been silent for centuries. They wouldn't—"

"They're not gone," Tyra interrupted, her voice growing more urgent. "They're here, somewhere, waiting."

Before Kade could respond, a low rumble echoed through the temple, shaking the very ground beneath their feet. Dust rained down from the ceiling, and the murals seemed to shift and warp in the dim light.

"We need to keep moving," Kade said, his hand tightening on his sword. "The sanctum is ahead."

They pressed on, moving deeper into the temple, the air growing colder with each step. Kade's heart pounded in his chest, his mind racing with memories of the day the gods had fallen. The betrayal that had begun here, in these very halls, haunted him still.

When they reached the sanctum, Kade paused at the entrance. The doors were carved with intricate patterns, depicting the gods in their final moments, their powers fading as they were struck down by an unseen force. Kade had seen this image countless times before, but now it seemed more ominous, more foreboding.

"We're close," Mira said, her voice barely a whisper. "The relic's location should be revealed here."

Kade pushed open the doors to the sanctum, revealing a vast chamber bathed in an eerie, dim light. At the center of the room stood an altar, and atop it lay a weathered scroll.

Tyra gasped as she approached the altar. "I've seen this before too... in my dreams."

Kade approached the altar, his hand trembling as he reached for the scroll. He hesitated, glancing back at his companions. They had come this far, but the truth of what lay ahead still eluded him.

With a deep breath, he unrolled the scroll.

The words written on it were ancient, barely legible, but Kade recognized them. They were the final words of the gods, a prophecy foretelling the rise of the ancient evil—and the one who would bring it forth.

"Kade," Mira said softly, "what does it say?"

Kade's grip tightened on the scroll, his heart sinking. "It says that the one who betrayed the gods will be the one to release the ancient evil... the one who bears their blood."

Mira's eyes widened in realization. "Your bloodline..."

Kade nodded, the weight of his guilt pressing down on him like never before. He had known, deep down, that his role in the gods' fall was far greater than he had ever admitted. But now, the truth was laid bare.

The gods had fallen because of him—and the ancient evil they had sealed away was tied to his very bloodline.

The sound of footsteps echoed from the far end of the chamber, and Kade looked up just in time to see a shadowy figure step into the light.

"Kade," the figure said, its voice cold and familiar. "It's time to finish what we started."

Kade's boots echoed ominously off the cracked stone floors as the group descended deeper into the Silent Temple. The air grew colder with each step, almost unnaturally so, as if the ancient stones themselves clung to a dying memory of some dark past. Their breaths came out in visible puffs, mist-like, vanishing into the oppressive darkness that enveloped the narrow passageways.

Tyra, who walked behind Kade, had grown silent since entering the temple. Her usual bravado and sharp remarks were absent, replaced by an eerie quiet. Kade glanced over his shoulder, his eyes narrowing at her pale face. She had been the one to insist she could hear voices earlier, claiming that the gods were speaking to her. Kade didn't believe it at first, but the temple had an unmistakable presence that even made him doubt his skepticism.

Mira, ever watchful, kept close to Tyra's side, her hand constantly hovering near the pouch where she kept her magical components. Kade caught the flicker of unease in Mira's eyes, though she hid it well beneath her calm facade. He knew she felt it too—the whisper of something ancient, buried, and yet very much awake.

The walls here were lined with faded murals, depicting long-forgotten deities in their moments of triumph. Kade remembered them all too well, the figures of the gods he once served—great and terrible in their power. His fingers brushed against the stone, feeling the worn grooves of one particular god, his former patron. He quickly withdrew his hand, the shame too much to bear.

At the front of the group, Sorin paused, the torchlight flickering as if responding to the unease in the air. "Something's wrong," he growled, his grip tightening on the hilt of his sword. Sorin was a man of action, not prone to fits of paranoia, which made his wariness all the more alarming.

Kade nodded in agreement. "We're not alone."

The deeper they ventured, the more unsettling the atmosphere became. The silence was broken only by their footfalls and the occasional creak of the ancient temple settling. But beneath the natural sounds, there was something more—an almost imperceptible whispering that seemed to rise from the very stones.

Tyra stopped abruptly, her hand gripping Kade's arm with surprising force. "Can't you hear it?" she whispered, her voice trembling. "The voices... They're getting louder."

Kade frowned, his eyes scanning the dimly lit corridor ahead. He strained his hearing, but all he could detect was the same faint whisper that had been present since they entered the temple. "What are they saying?" he asked cautiously, though part of him wasn't sure he wanted to know.

Tyra's eyes glazed over as she focused on the voices only she could hear. "They're... they're calling for help. Begging to be freed. The gods... they're trapped."

Mira stepped forward, her brow furrowed. "Tyra, be careful. The temple is a place of great power, but it's also a place of great deception. The gods have been silent for centuries. Whatever you're hearing may not be what it seems."

Tyra looked at her with wide eyes. "I know what I'm hearing, Mira. They're real. They're here."

Kade exchanged a glance with Mira, concern tightening in his chest. There were countless legends about temples like this one, places where the divine and the profane crossed paths. But those stories usually ended in madness for those who listened too closely to the voices.

"Stay close," Kade ordered, his voice harsher than intended. He couldn't afford to lose control of the group—not now, not when they were so close to their goal. "We're almost to the inner sanctum. Whatever's down here, we'll face it together."

The entrance to the sanctum loomed ahead, a massive stone door adorned with the faded sigils of the fallen gods. Kade hesitated for a moment, memories of his past flooding back with a vengeance. This was where it had all begun—the place where he had committed the ultimate betrayal. He had stood before this very door, weapon in hand, and allowed the unthinkable to happen.

Mira noticed his hesitation. "Kade, are you alright?"

He shook his head, forcing the memories back into the recesses of his mind. "I'll be fine."

With a deep breath, Kade pushed against the door, his muscles straining as it groaned open. A cold gust of wind rushed out from the darkness beyond, carrying with it a sense of foreboding that chilled him to the bone. The room beyond was vast, its ceiling disappearing into shadows, and at its center was an altar, ancient and crumbling, covered in the dust of centuries.

Sorin stepped forward, his eyes scanning the room with practiced caution. "This doesn't feel right," he muttered. "I don't like it."

Tyra's voice came out in a whisper, barely audible. "They're here. The gods... they're watching us."

Kade glanced at the girl, but before he could say anything, Mira let out a sharp gasp. "Look!"

Kade followed her gaze to the far wall, where a series of intricate carvings adorned the stone. At first glance, they appeared to be more depictions of the gods, but as he looked closer, he realized they were something far more sinister. The figures on the wall were not gods, but twisted, malevolent beings—things that had no place in the natural order of the world.

"Demons," Kade whispered, his throat dry.

Mira nodded grimly. "Or worse. This temple wasn't just a place of worship. It was a prison."

As the group approached the altar, Tyra's behavior became more erratic. She muttered under her breath, her eyes darting around as if trying to track invisible presences. Kade could feel the tension building, an invisible weight pressing down on them from all sides.

"We need to find the clue and get out of here," Sorin said, his voice low. "This place is wrong. It's dangerous."

Kade nodded in agreement. He stepped closer to the altar, his eyes scanning the inscriptions that lined its surface. There was something familiar about them—something he had seen before during his time with the Holy Order. But before he could make sense of the writing, a sudden pulse of dark energy surged through the room, sending him stumbling backward.

The air grew thick, and a low, guttural voice echoed from the shadows. "You dare disturb the sanctum of the Fallen."

Tyra screamed, clutching her head as the voices grew louder, more insistent. "They're angry! They want to be freed!"

Kade drew his sword, his eyes darting around the room. "We've got company."

From the shadows, figures began to emerge—twisted, misshapen creatures, their eyes glowing with an unnatural light. They moved silently, their forms flickering as if they weren't fully real, yet Kade knew they were dangerous.

Mira quickly began weaving a spell, her hands moving in intricate patterns as she summoned her magic. Sorin stepped forward, his sword raised, ready to fight.

"Kade!" Mira shouted, her voice strained. "We need to close whatever portal is bringing these things through!"

Kade's mind raced. The altar. It had to be the source. But how could they close it?

As the creatures closed in, Tyra collapsed to the floor, writhing in pain as the voices overwhelmed her. "I can't—" she gasped, "I can't stop them!"

Kade rushed to her side, grabbing her by the shoulders. "Tyra, listen to me. You have to focus. Block them out!"

Tears streamed down her face as she shook her head. "I can't... They're too strong..."

Kade cursed under his breath. There had to be a way to stop this, to seal whatever was allowing these creatures to manifest. His eyes flicked to the inscriptions on the altar. They were a ritual of some kind—something ancient, powerful.

"Kade!" Sorin shouted, swinging his sword at one of the creatures. "Do something!"

With a burst of determination, Kade knelt before the altar, his hands tracing the carvings. He could feel the dark magic pulsing beneath the surface, like a heartbeat, steady and unrelenting. This was no simple lock to be sealed with brute force. It would take something more.

Mira, seeing what Kade was attempting, began to channel her own magic into the altar. "I'll buy you time," she muttered, her voice filled with strain.

Kade closed his eyes and concentrated, his mind reaching back to his time in the Holy Order. He had learned the rites of the gods, but this... this was different. He could feel the dark energy resisting him, pushing back against his will.

The creatures were closing in, their twisted forms growing more solid with every passing moment. Sorin fought valiantly, but he was outnumbered, his sword barely keeping the creatures at bay.

Kade gritted his teeth. "I won't let them win again," he growled, his voice filled with resolve.

He poured everything he had into the inscriptions, willing the portal to close. The dark energy surged, resisting him at every turn, but he refused to give in. This was his chance for redemption, his chance to right the wrongs of the past.

With a final push, the altar glowed with a brilliant light, and the creatures let out an unholy scream as they began to fade, their forms dissolving into the air.

The room fell silent once more, the oppressive weight lifting as the last of the creatures vanished. Tyra lay on the floor, her breathing shallow but steady. Sorin, bloodied but alive, lowered his sword, his eyes filled with relief.

Mira collapsed to her knees, exhausted from the effort. "It's... over," she whispered, though her voice carried a note of uncertainty.

Kade stood slowly, his hands still trembling from the strain. He had sealed the portal, but the temple was far from safe. There were still secrets buried here—secrets that could destroy them if they weren't careful.

"We need to leave," he said quietly, his voice filled with grim determination. "This place... it's not what we thought."

Sorin nodded, wiping the blood from his blade. "Let's get out of here."

As they turned to leave, Tyra spoke, her voice weak but determined. "They're not gone," she whispered. "The gods... they're still trapped."

Kade glanced at her, his expression unreadable. He had come here seeking redemption, but now he realized that the temple held more than just the ghosts of his past. There were forces at work here that were beyond his understanding—forces that had been waiting for centuries to be unleashed.

And Kade knew, deep down, that their journey was far from over.

As the group made their way back through the temple, Kade's mind raced. He had sealed the portal, but something told him that this was just the beginning. The gods were still silent, but their presence lingered, like a shadow that refused to fade.

Kade couldn't shake the feeling that they had awakened something ancient and dangerous—something that would follow them, no matter how far they ran.

And as they stepped out into the light of the setting sun, Kade knew one thing for certain: the Silent Temple had been a prison, but it was also a warning.

A warning that the gods, once silent, were beginning to stir.

Chapter 3: The Broken Kingdom

The once-glorious capital of Rethnor, now a shadow of its former self, lay sprawled beneath the twilight sky. The sun, sinking below the horizon, cast long, eerie shadows across the shattered remnants of a city that had once been the heart of an empire. What had been a beacon of prosperity and grandeur now resembled a graveyard, its streets strewn with debris and remnants of a bygone era. The spires that had once touched the heavens were now fractured, their silhouettes a stark reminder of the empire's fall.

Kade, Mira, Tyra, and Sorin stood on the edge of the city's ruins, their eyes taking in the desolate landscape. The acrid smell of smoke and decay hung heavy in the air, mingling with the faint scent of blood that seemed to seep from every corner of the city. The devastation was both physical and emotional, a reflection of the chaos that had engulfed the entire empire.

"We should find shelter," Mira suggested, her voice barely carrying over the distant sounds of conflict. Her eyes scanned the ruins, taking in the shattered remains of buildings and the occasional flicker of movement in the distance. The city was a labyrinth of danger, and finding a safe place was imperative.

Kade nodded, his gaze fixed on the distant silhouette of what had once been a grand palace. "The next clue to the Crown's location should be here," he said with grim determination. His words were more a statement of fact than hope. The journey to this broken city had been long and fraught with peril, and the stakes had never been higher.

As they ventured deeper into the city, the reality of its situation became increasingly apparent. The once-bustling streets were now a battleground, with various factions clashing for control over the remains of the capital. Skirmishes erupted sporadically, and the city's inhabitants navigated a precarious balance of shifting allegiances and constant danger. The chaos was palpable, the atmosphere charged with the remnants of countless conflicts.

Tyra, her keen senses attuned to the environment, gestured toward a narrow alleyway. "That might be a good place to find temporary refuge," she said, her voice low and urgent. The alleyway was partially concealed by a tattered curtain, its entrance hidden from casual view. Kade, Mira, and Sorin followed her lead, moving cautiously toward the entrance.

Inside, the alleyway led to a small, dilapidated building. Its wooden door hung precariously on its hinges, creaking as Kade pushed it open. The interior was dimly lit, the air thick with dust and the musty smell of abandonment. Broken furniture and scattered debris littered the floor, a stark reminder of the building's forsaken state.

Kade's gaze swept over the room, noting the layers of dust that covered every surface. A lone table in the center of the room was cluttered with maps, documents, and various artifacts. The disarray suggested that someone had recently been here, and Kade's instincts told him that the information on the table could be valuable.

Mira approached the table and began sifting through the papers. Her eyes scanned the maps and documents with a mixture of curiosity and concern. "These maps... they seem to detail the city's layout and various power struggles," she observed. Her fingers traced the intricate markings and annotations, trying to decipher their significance.

Kade surveyed the room, his thoughts racing as he considered their next move. "We need to find someone who knows this city well," he said, his voice filled with determination. "We can't navigate this chaos on our own. We need someone who can guide us and help us locate the next clue."

As if in response to Kade's words, the sound of footsteps echoed from the hallway outside. The group tensed, their senses on high alert. Kade's hand instinctively moved toward the hilt of his sword. The door to the building creaked open, and a figure appeared in the doorway, cloaked in a dark robe with a hood that obscured their face.

"Who goes there?" the figure demanded, their voice low and commanding. The tone carried an air of authority and suspicion, and Kade could sense that this was not someone to be trifled with.

Kade stepped forward, his posture defensive but not aggressive. "We're not here to cause trouble," he said, trying to keep his voice calm. "We're seeking information on the Crown of the Fallen. We mean no harm."

The figure's eyes, though hidden in the shadow of the hood, seemed to scrutinize Kade intently. "You seek the

Crown?" the figure repeated, a hint of incredulity in their voice. "Many have come before you, drawn by its promise of power and salvation. Few have succeeded."

Mira, sensing the figure's hesitation, stepped forward. "We have no interest in the politics of this city. We're here for a purpose greater than ourselves. We're trying to uncover the truth behind the Crown's location."

The figure's stance relaxed slightly, and they stepped into the room fully, revealing a face marked by years of hardship and wisdom. The eyes beneath the hood were sharp and knowing. "Very well," the figure said after a moment's consideration. "If you are truly seeking the truth, then you must prove your intentions are genuine. I may be able to help, but first, you must assist me."

Kade's brow furrowed in curiosity. "Assist you with what?"

The figure reached into their robe and produced a small, intricately carved box. "This is the key to an ancient vault hidden beneath the city," they explained. "Inside the vault are records that may shed light on the Crown's whereabouts. However, the vault has been seized by one of the rival factions."

Mira examined the box closely, her eyes narrowing with interest. "What makes this vault so significant?"

The figure's gaze grew serious. "The vault holds knowledge and artifacts from before the fall of the gods," they explained. "It may contain clues about the Crown or the forces that seek to control it. Recovering this key is crucial."

Kade considered the offer, weighing the potential risks against the possible rewards. "We'll help you retrieve the vault," he said finally. "But in return, you must guide us through the city and provide us with the information we need."

The figure nodded in agreement. "Very well. Follow me."

The group followed the figure through the maze of ruined streets and alleyways, their path illuminated only by the dim light of their torches. The city was a chaotic blend of conflicts and negotiations, and every step was fraught with danger. Kade kept his senses sharp, aware that any moment could bring a confrontation with one of the rival factions.

The figure led them to a dilapidated building, its exterior almost indistinguishable from the surrounding ruins. The entrance was concealed behind a hidden panel in the wall, which the figure revealed with practiced ease. They descended into the darkness below, entering a network of underground passages that stretched far beneath the city.

The air grew colder and more oppressive as they made their way deeper into the underground labyrinth. The sense of impending danger was palpable, and Kade could feel the weight of their mission pressing down on him.

At the end of one of the passages, they arrived at a heavy, iron-bound door. The figure produced a key and unlocked it, revealing a dimly lit chamber filled with shelves of dusty scrolls and ancient artifacts. The vault was a treasure trove of forgotten knowledge, its walls lined with records from a time long past.

Kade's eyes scanned the room, taking in the sight of the ancient texts and relics. The vault was a place of immense historical and possibly magical significance. If the rumors about the Crown were true, this place could hold the key to finding it.

The figure moved with purpose, retrieving a large, ornate tome from one of the shelves. "This is what we need," they said, holding up the tome. "It contains records of the ancient gods and their power."

Mira, who had been examining some of the documents on the table, looked up with a sense of excitement. "This could be the breakthrough we need," she said. "But we have to be quick. We don't know how long we'll have before the rival factions discover our presence."

Kade nodded in agreement. "We need to move. Gather what you can and let's get out of here."

As they prepared to leave the vault, the sound of footsteps echoed from the passageway, growing louder with each passing moment. Kade's heart raced as he realized they were not alone. The rival factions had discovered their presence and were closing in.

"Get ready," Kade ordered, his voice urgent. "We need to move quickly."

The group gathered their belongings and made their way back through the labyrinth of passages. The underground network was a maze, and every turn seemed to lead them deeper into the heart of the city. The sense of urgency grew with each step as they navigated the dangerous terrain.

Emerging from the underground, they were met with the sight of the ruined city in its full desolation. The distant sounds of conflict grew louder, and the realization that they were still in a volatile and dangerous environment was sobering. The rival factions were out in force, and the city was a chaotic battleground.

Kade and his companions fought their way through the streets, their skills and determination guiding them as they evaded their pursuers. The struggle was fierce, but their resolve remained unshaken. The knowledge they had gained was crucial, and they could not afford to lose it.

Eventually, they reached the safety of a hidden alcove, a secluded spot in the ruins where they could regroup and assess their situation. The tension of the pursuit was evident in their faces, and the weight of their mission hung heavily on their shoulders.

Kade took a deep breath, his mind racing as he considered their next move. "We've retrieved the records," he said, his voice filled with resolve. "Now we need to decipher them and find the next clue."

The figure who had guided them through the city remained silent, their eyes fixed on the tome they had recovered. The journey was far from over, and the challenges ahead were only beginning. But with the knowledge they had gained and the strength of their resolve, Kade and his companions were prepared to face whatever lay ahead.

The ruins of Rethnor stood as a testament to the city's fall and the trials that awaited those who sought to uncover its secrets. As Kade and his companions set out on their next quest, the promise of uncovering the truth behind the Crown and restoring balance to their world guided their every step.

The road ahead was fraught with danger, but with each step, they drew closer to their goal. The journey through the broken kingdom was only beginning, and the path to redemption and truth was paved with the remnants of the past.

The once-great capital of Rethnor lay in a state of disrepair, its majestic spires now crumbling, and its once-bustling streets now echoing with the distant sounds of conflict. The city's heart had been hollowed out by the ongoing struggle for power among the factions that now fought for control. Kade and his companions moved cautiously through the ruined cityscape, their every step laden with tension as they sought the next clue to the Crown's whereabouts.

The sun was a dim, feeble light through the haze of smoke that lingered over the city. Mira's eyes darted around, her senses heightened as she scanned for any sign of danger. Tyra, always alert, was in the lead, her nimble frame weaving through the debris with practiced ease. Sorin followed closely, his heavy armor clinking softly with each step. Kade, however, lagged behind, his gaze fixed on the shattered remnants of a once-proud empire.

Their objective was clear: find the next lead in their quest for the Crown of the Fallen. Yet, as they ventured deeper into the city, it became apparent that their task was fraught with more peril than they had anticipated. The political machinations of the warring factions were as treacherous as the physical dangers that lurked around every corner.

As they approached what appeared to be a marketplace, the remnants of a once-vibrant trade hub, Kade felt a chill run down his spine. The market was deserted, save for a few scavengers picking through the wreckage. It was here that Kade's mind wandered back to his past, to the time when Rethnor was a beacon of civilization rather than a ruin. His thoughts were interrupted by a sudden commotion.

A loud crash and shouts echoed from a nearby building. Kade's instincts kicked in, and he signaled for the group to take cover. They moved swiftly, finding refuge behind a crumbling wall. Peering through a gap, they saw a skirmish unfolding in the street. A group of ragtag soldiers clashed with a well-armed faction, their combat echoing with the clang of steel and the roar of defiant cries.

The battle was chaotic, a stark reminder of the lawlessness that had overtaken the city. It was clear that the factions were not just fighting for territory but for control of whatever remnants of power could be salvaged from the ruins. Amid the chaos, Kade's gaze was drawn to a familiar figure, standing on a makeshift platform and shouting orders. The figure was clad in ornate armor that marked him as a leader—a leader Kade recognized all too well.

"Sevran," Kade muttered under his breath, his face paling. The name came with a heavy weight, a reminder of past betrayals and broken oaths.

Sevran, a former ally and rival, was one of the key figures who had orchestrated Kade's downfall. Their past encounters were marked by a complex web of friendship and enmity, culminating in the fall of Kade's order. Sevran's appearance in Rethnor was no mere coincidence; it was a manifestation of the personal vendetta that had haunted Kade for years.

As the battle raged on, Kade's internal conflict deepened. He could not ignore the chance to confront Sevran and potentially gain information about the Crown's location. But the risks were considerable. Revealing himself could draw unwanted attention to the group and jeopardize their quest.

"Mira, Tyra, Sorin," Kade whispered, pulling his companions close. "We need to get closer to Sevran. He might have information about the Crown or lead us to someone who does. But we must be careful; if he sees me..."

Mira nodded, her face set with determination. "We'll need a diversion. Something to draw attention away from us while we make our move."

Tyra's eyes glinted with a mischievous spark. "Leave that to me. I know a few tricks that might come in handy."

Sorin, his expression grim, gripped his sword tightly. "We should act quickly. The longer we wait, the more dangerous this situation becomes."

With their plan in place, Tyra slipped into the shadows, preparing her diversion. Mira and Sorin moved to flank Sevran's position, while Kade steeled himself for the confrontation. The air was thick with tension as the battle continued to rage around them, a chaotic backdrop to their dangerous mission.

Tyra's diversion was effective. She triggered a series of loud explosions that sent several of Sevran's soldiers scattering, creating a temporary lull in the skirmish. This provided Kade and his companions with the opportunity they needed to move closer to Sevran.

Kade's heart pounded as he approached Sevran's position. The former ally was now completely absorbed in coordinating his forces, his back turned. Kade's resolve hardened. This was his chance to confront the man who had played a significant role in his downfall.

"Kade," Sevran's voice cut through the chaos, his tone filled with surprise and malice. "I should have known you would come crawling back."

Kade stepped forward, his face a mask of cold determination. "Sevran. I see you're still making a mess of things. I'm here for the Crown. Tell me what you know."

Sevran's eyes narrowed, a predatory smile crossing his lips. "The Crown? You're still obsessed with that relic? You must be desperate to be willing to face me."

The two men stood facing each other, their shared history hanging between them like a heavy shroud. Sevran's words dripped with contempt, a stark reminder of the betrayal that had shattered Kade's life.

"You know more than you're letting on," Kade said, his voice steady. "What have you done with the Crown?"

Sevran's expression darkened. "The Crown is not something you should be concerned about. It's tied to forces far beyond your understanding."

Kade's frustration flared. "You were always one to play games, Sevran. If you have any information, you'd better share it now."

Sevran's gaze shifted to the battlefield around them. "You're a fool if you think you can simply take what you want. There are things at play here that you can't begin to comprehend. The Crown is just a piece of a much larger puzzle."

The conversation was abruptly interrupted by the arrival of a new group of soldiers, their presence shifting the dynamics of the confrontation. Sevran's attention was diverted, and Kade realized that their time was running out.

"We're done here," Kade said, turning to leave. "If you have any information, now's your chance to give it."

Sevran's eyes followed Kade with a mixture of anger and amusement. "You think you're in control? The truth will come out soon enough. Until then, you're nothing but a pawn in a much bigger game."

With that, Kade and his companions retreated, slipping back into the shadows of the ruined city. The encounter had been both revealing and unsettling. Sevran's cryptic remarks hinted at deeper secrets, but they had gained no concrete information about the Crown's location.

As they regrouped in a nearby safehouse, Kade's mind raced with the implications of their meeting. The revelation that Sevran was involved in a larger, more complex scheme was troubling. It suggested that the quest for the Crown was entangled in a web of deceit and power struggles that extended far beyond their initial understanding.

Mira's expression was thoughtful as she studied Kade. "What did you learn from Sevran? Was there anything useful?"

Kade shook his head, his frustration evident. "He's as elusive as ever. But he made it clear that there's more to the Crown than we realized. He spoke of a larger game, and I'm beginning to think that we're only scratching the surface of what's really at stake."

Tyra, still catching her breath from her diversion, added, "So, what's our next move? We need to stay ahead of these factions and find out what Sevran was really talking about."

Sorin, ever the pragmatic warrior, nodded in agreement. "We need to stay focused. The Crown is our primary objective, but we can't ignore the possibility that there are others with their own agendas. We need to be cautious."

As the sun dipped below the horizon, casting long shadows over the ruins of Rethnor, the weight of their mission pressed heavily on Kade and his companions. The city's broken remnants stood as a stark reminder of the challenges they faced.

The path to the Crown was fraught with danger and deception, and their journey was far from over.

With the revelations about Sevran's involvement and the looming threat of the ancient evil tied to Kade's bloodline, the quest for the Crown had become more perilous than ever. The road ahead was uncertain, but Kade and his companions were determined to press on, knowing that the fate of their world depended on their success.

As they prepared to continue their search, Kade's thoughts turned to the legacy of his past and the choices that lay ahead. The journey was shaping up to be a test of both their strength and their resolve, and the stakes had never been higher. The shattered kingdom of Rethnor held many secrets, and the quest for the Crown was only the beginning of a larger, more dangerous game.

Chapter 4: The Hunt Begins

The dawn of the day found the ragtag group of Kade's companions huddled beneath a crumbling overhang, their breath mingling with the frost of the morning. The sun struggled to pierce the thick blanket of clouds that hung over the desolate landscape of the mountain pass. A chill wind howled around them, carrying whispers of danger and the promise of treachery.

Kade paced back and forth, his heavy boots stirring up small clouds of dust and frost from the rocky ground. His mind was consumed by thoughts of their journey and the impending encounter with the outlaws who controlled the pass. The group had no choice but to seek their help to traverse the treacherous terrain that lay ahead.

Mira sat cross-legged on a nearby boulder, her eyes closed in meditation. Her long, dark hair cascaded over her shoulders, and she seemed utterly disconnected from the chaos surrounding them. Tyra, the young thief, was hunched over a small campfire, warming her hands while casting occasional glances at Kade. Sorin, the burly mercenary with a perpetual scowl, sharpened his blade with meticulous care, the rasp of metal against stone a constant background noise.

Kade stopped his pacing and turned to face his companions. "We need to make sure everyone understands what's at stake," he said, his voice carrying the weight of authority. "The outlaws are not to be underestimated. They are as ruthless as they are cunning."

Tyra looked up from the fire, her eyes bright with determination. "I've heard stories about these outlaws. They're not just bandits; they're organized and dangerous. What's the plan, Kade?"

Kade's gaze shifted to Mira, who had opened her eyes and was now regarding him with an inscrutable expression. "We need to strike a deal with them," Kade replied. "Our objective is to negotiate safe passage through the pass. But we must be cautious. The outlaws will want something in return, and it's likely to be costly."

Mira nodded slowly, her expression thoughtful. "Do you think they'll honor any deal we make? Or will they try to double-cross us?"

Sorin finished sharpening his blade and joined the conversation. "In my experience, outlaws keep their word only when it's beneficial for them. If we can make them see the advantage of helping us, they might cooperate."

Kade's gaze turned to the mountain pass in the distance, a narrow and winding route that snaked its way through the jagged peaks. "We don't have the luxury of time. The outlaws are likely already aware of our presence. We must proceed with caution and be prepared to make concessions."

The group fell into silence, each member lost in their own thoughts as they prepared for the upcoming encounter. The wind howled louder, as if in anticipation of the confrontation to come.

As the day wore on, the sky grew darker, and the temperature dropped even further. The group packed up their meager supplies and began the trek toward the heart of the mountain pass. The path was treacherous, with steep inclines and loose rocks that threatened to send them tumbling down the slopes.

After several hours of arduous climbing, they finally reached the entrance to the outlaw stronghold, a hidden valley concealed by the rugged terrain. The valley was surrounded by makeshift fortifications, with crude wooden palisades and watchtowers. The sound of clanging metal and distant voices indicated the presence of a well-organized camp.

Kade signaled for the group to halt. They were concealed behind a large boulder, peering out at the scene before them. A group of armed men and women moved about the camp, their movements purposeful and disciplined. They were clearly a well-trained force.

Mira leaned in closer to Kade, her voice barely a whisper. "We need to approach them carefully. If we're too aggressive, we might provoke them into hostility."

Kade nodded in agreement. "I'll handle the initial negotiations. The rest of you stay alert and be ready to act if things go south."

With that, Kade stepped out from behind the boulder and began making his way toward the camp. The outlaws' watchful eyes immediately turned toward him, their expressions a mix of curiosity and suspicion.

As Kade approached the camp, a tall, imposing figure emerged from the shadows. The outlaw leader, a man with a weathered face and a scar running across his cheek, regarded Kade with a steely gaze. He was flanked by several armed guards, their weapons at the ready.

"State your business," the outlaw leader demanded, his voice gruff and commanding.

Kade took a deep breath and met the leader's gaze with unwavering resolve. "I am Kade, a warrior on a quest of great importance. I seek safe passage through your territory. In return, I am prepared to offer you something of value."

The outlaw leader's eyes narrowed. "And why should we trust you? What makes you think we need what you have to offer?"

Kade's mind raced as he considered his next move. "I know of a treasure, a relic of immense power. It is something that could greatly benefit your organization. But I need your help to reach my destination."

The leader's eyes flickered with interest. "A treasure, you say? And what makes you think we would be willing to make a deal with you?"

Kade took a step closer, his voice dropping to a conspiratorial tone. "I know of a cache of ancient artifacts hidden in the ruins of an old temple. It is said to hold great power, but it is heavily guarded. I can guide you to it if you agree to assist us in crossing the pass."

The leader's expression remained inscrutable, but Kade could see a glimmer of calculation in his eyes. "You have a deal," the leader said finally. "But we will accompany you and ensure that you don't try to deceive us. If you betray us, the consequences will be severe."

Kade nodded, relief washing over him. "Agreed. We will keep our end of the bargain."

The outlaw leader signaled for his men to prepare, and soon the camp was abuzz with activity as they readied themselves for the journey. Kade returned to his companions, who were waiting anxiously.

"Everything's set," Kade announced. "We have the outlaws' help, but we must be vigilant. They will be watching us closely."

Mira, Tyra, and Sorin nodded, their expressions a mix of relief and apprehension. The group fell into line as the outlaws led them through the mountain pass, their footsteps echoing in the cold air.

The path ahead was fraught with danger, and the group knew that their journey through the pass would be a test of their resolve. But for now, they had secured the aid they needed and were one step closer to their goal.

As they moved deeper into the pass, the sky grew darker, and the wind howled with a mournful wail. The journey ahead would be fraught with challenges, but Kade and his companions were determined to see it through, no matter the cost.

The mountain pass loomed ahead, a jagged scar against the horizon. The air grew colder and thinner as Kade and his companions trekked up the narrow, winding path, flanked by sheer cliffs and treacherous drops. The once-verdant landscape had given way to a harsh, unforgiving terrain where even the smallest misstep could mean death. The group trudged on, their breath forming visible clouds in the freezing air.

The outlaws had been true to their word, providing them with a guide through the pass—a wiry man with a hood pulled low over his eyes and a silent demeanor that belied his sharp instincts. His presence was unsettling, adding an additional layer of tension to their already fraught journey. Each member of Kade's party seemed to be lost in their own thoughts, the weight of the quest pressing heavily on their shoulders.

Tyra, ever perceptive, fell back slightly to walk beside Mira, who had been unusually quiet since their encounter with the outlaws. "You've been distant," Tyra remarked softly, her voice nearly lost in the howling wind. "Something's bothering you."

Mira glanced at her, her eyes hidden behind a veil of shadow cast by her hood. "Just thinking," she said, her voice tinged with an unspoken melancholy. "It's not easy to keep secrets from people who've trusted me."

Tyra tilted her head. "Secrets? What do you mean?"

Mira's expression hardened, but she forced a faint smile. "It's nothing, really. Just the weight of our task. The Crown of the Fallen... it means more than we know."

Tyra's curiosity was piqued. "What do you know about it?"

Mira hesitated, then said, "More than I've let on. My family—my ancestors—they were among the last to serve the gods before their fall. There's a prophecy that's been passed down, one that speaks of a time when the Crown would be sought. It's said that whoever claims it will bring about a reckoning."

Tyra's eyes widened. "And what does it say about what happens if the Crown is found?"

Mira's gaze fell to the ground. "It's unclear. But it suggests that the one who seeks it will be tested in ways they can't imagine. The gods themselves... they are a forgotten dream, but their power lingers in the Crown."

Tyra's mind raced. "So, you're saying that this quest might lead us to something far darker than we've anticipated?"

Mira nodded slowly. "Perhaps. I've seen too much to believe in simple salvation anymore. The gods' fall wasn't just a loss of power; it was the release of something ancient and terrible. I fear the Crown might be the key to that power."

The conversation ended as abruptly as it had started, with Mira turning away, her gaze fixed on the treacherous path ahead. The shadows of the mountains loomed like dark sentinels, and the wind's mournful cry seemed to echo the foreboding of their journey.

As the day wore on, the mountain pass grew increasingly perilous. The guide led them to a narrow ledge where a makeshift camp was set up by the outlaws. The camp was crude but functional, with a fire pit in the center and a few rudimentary shelters made from rough-hewn wood and animal hides.

The outlaws were a rough lot, their faces hardened by the harsh life of the mountains. They eyed Kade and his companions with a mixture of suspicion and grudging respect. One of them, a burly man with a scar running down his left cheek, approached Kade as he and the group gathered around the fire.

"Evening," the man grunted, his voice rough like gravel. "You'll need to make a sacrifice if you want to pass through the pass safely."

Kade frowned. "A sacrifice?"

The man nodded, his gaze steely. "Our ways are our own. You give us something of value, and we'll make sure you reach your destination without trouble."

Kade exchanged glances with his companions. The group had little to offer, save for the supplies they carried and their weapons. But as the outlaws' eyes turned calculating, Kade knew they would need to comply to avoid conflict.

Tyra stepped forward, her eyes gleaming with a determination that masked her anxiety. "I have something," she said, pulling out a small, intricately carved box from her pack. "It's a family heirloom. It's valuable, and I'm willing to trade it for safe passage."

The outlaws' eyes widened at the sight of the box, and the burly man's expression softened slightly. "A fine piece," he said, reaching out to inspect it. "This will do."

With the exchange made, the outlaws kept their word, guiding Kade's group through the pass without incident. As they continued their journey, Mira's silence grew more pronounced, and Kade couldn't help but sense an undercurrent of tension between her and the others.

The night was long and cold, the fire crackling weakly against the oppressive chill. As Kade lay on his bedroll, staring up at the starless sky, his mind was awash with the weight of their quest. The vision of the Crown haunted his dreams, a golden artifact that seemed to pulse with a malevolent light. He was no closer to understanding its true nature, but the shadows of his past and the impending danger loomed larger with each passing hour.

In the early hours of the morning, Kade was jolted awake by a commotion. The outlaws were stirring, their voices raised in urgent whispers. Kade quickly gathered his belongings and joined his companions, who were already alert and ready for action.

The burly outlaw leader stood at the edge of the camp, his face pale. "There's something wrong," he said, his voice tight with fear. "We've sensed an unnatural presence in the mountains. It's as if something is stirring in the depths."

Mira's eyes narrowed. "Unnatural presence? What do you mean?"

The outlaw's gaze flicked to the shadows of the mountain pass. "We've felt it before, but never this close. It's as if something ancient is awakening."

Kade felt a shiver run down his spine. The weight of Mira's earlier warning and the burden of his own secrets pressed heavily on him. The ancient evil tied to his bloodline seemed to be closing in, and the Crown's dark influence was becoming more palpable with each passing day.

The group readied themselves for the journey ahead, their resolve steeling as they prepared to face whatever lay beyond the mountain pass. The shadows of the past, the mysteries of the Crown, and the dangers of the treacherous terrain all converged, creating a volatile mix that would test their strength and unity.

As the first light of dawn broke over the horizon, casting a cold, gray light over the pass, Kade led his companions forward. The path ahead was fraught with uncertainty, and the quest for the Crown had become not just a journey through a physical landscape, but a descent into the heart of darkness that threatened to consume them all.

Chapter 5: The Wasteland of Ash

The sun had scarcely begun its descent when Kade and his companions emerged from the mountain pass into the Ashen Desert. The shift in landscape was jarring, as if they had crossed a threshold from one world into another. Where the jagged peaks had loomed dark and oppressive, the desert now stretched out before them in a vast, scorching expanse.

The air was heavy with the acrid stench of sulfur, the sky above a relentless sheet of gray. This wasteland was once the site of epic battles—tales of gods and men clashing in conflicts that had scarred the land deeply. Now, it was a barren expanse where the remnants of ancient flames lingered in the dry wind, the ground underfoot cracked and desolate.

Kade scanned the horizon, his face shielded from the grit by a tattered cloth. He could barely make out the contours of distant hills, their silhouettes smudged by the haze. The heat was oppressive, and the air seemed to shimmer with every step they took.

"Keep close," Kade commanded, his voice strained but authoritative. "We need to move swiftly through this wasteland. The storms here are unpredictable and dangerous."

Mira nodded, her expression stoic despite the harsh environment. She had wrapped herself in a hooded cloak, her eyes scanning the desert for signs of trouble. Tyra, ever the enigma, seemed unperturbed by the heat, her small frame darting ahead with a fluid grace that seemed to counter the desert's harshness. Sorin, the grizzled mercenary, trudged alongside Kade, his heavy armor clinking with every step.

As they pressed forward, the sand seemed to shift beneath them, the heat making the ground unstable. Kade's thoughts drifted back to the Silent Temple, where they had uncovered fragments of an old prophecy. He could still feel the unsettling presence of the dark entity that had lingered there. The prophecy spoke of trials ahead, trials that would test not just their strength but their very sanity.

Their first night in the desert was marked by the eerie silence that blanketed the wasteland. As darkness fell, the temperature plummeted, and a biting cold replaced the earlier heat. They set up a small camp, using what little wood they could find to start a fire. Its flickering light cast long shadows that danced ominously on the surrounding dunes.

"How much further to the next landmark?" Mira asked, breaking the silence. Her voice was barely above a whisper, as if speaking too loudly might summon some unseen danger.

Kade consulted the map he had retrieved from the Silent Temple. The map was ancient, its surface weathered and fragile, marked with runes sand symbols that had been interpreted as guiding their way through the desert.

"According to this, we should reach the Oasis of the Fallen by dawn," Kade replied. "If the map is accurate, it will be a small reprieve from this hellish landscape."

Tyra, who had been scanning the horizon, turned back with a frown. "I've been having these... visions," she admitted, her voice trembling slightly. "The desert seems to be showing me things—images of fire and shadows. It's like the land itself is trying to speak to me."

Mira's eyes narrowed, a hint of concern in her gaze. "Visions? What kind of visions?"

"Fire and shadows," Tyra repeated. "I see the Crown of the Fallen, but it's always shrouded in darkness, as if it's already corrupted."

Kade exchanged a worried glance with Mira. The visions were troubling, but they had little choice but to press on. "We'll need to stay alert," Kade said. "The desert has a way of playing tricks on the mind. It might be nothing, or it might be a sign of something more sinister."

As the night wore on, the fire cast a weak glow against the encroaching darkness. The desert's silence was occasionally broken by the distant howl of a creature or the unsettling rustle of wind through the sand. The companions huddled close to the fire, their faces illuminated by its faint light.

Kade found it difficult to sleep, his mind racing with thoughts of the ancient prophecy and the task that lay ahead. The wasteland seemed to pulse with a malevolent energy, as if the land itself was aware of their presence and intent on thwarting their quest.

In the early hours of the morning, just before dawn, Kade was jolted awake by a series of sharp, metallic clangs. He leapt to his feet, instinctively reaching for his sword, but found Sorin already on alert, his eyes scanning the darkness.

"What is it?" Kade demanded.

Sorin pointed towards the edge of their camp. "Something's coming."

The companions scrambled to their feet, eyes straining to see through the dark. The distant sound of approaching footsteps became clearer, and the figure of a rider emerged from the gloom. The rider was cloaked in a heavy robe, their face hidden beneath a hood. The horse they rode was skeletal, its ribs jutting out beneath its skin.

The rider approached with deliberate slowness, the sand swirling around them like a living thing. As they drew nearer, the hooded figure raised a hand, and the desert's winds seemed to still.

"Who goes there?" Kade called out, his voice firm despite the unease gnawing at him.

The rider halted a few paces from the campfire, their voice a low, rasping whisper. "Travelers in the wasteland, seeking the Crown."

Kade's grip tightened on his sword. "And you are?"

"A guide," the rider said. "The desert is a harsh and unforgiving place. I offer my services for a price."

Kade exchanged glances with Mira and Sorin. They had little choice but to trust this mysterious figure, for the desert's dangers were too great to face alone.

"What's the price?" Mira asked, her tone cautious.

The rider's hood shifted slightly, revealing a pair of piercing eyes that glowed faintly in the firelight. "A story. Tell me of your quest, and I will lead you to the Oasis of the Fallen."

Kade hesitated, weighing the risks of divulging their mission against the immediate need for guidance. In the end, he nodded, signaling his agreement. "Very well. We seek the

Crown of the Fallen, an artifact of immense power. Our journey is perilous, and we need all the help we can get."

The rider listened in silence, their eyes never leaving Kade's. When he had finished, the rider nodded once, as if satisfied.

"Then follow me," the rider said, turning their horse and leading the way.

The group packed up their camp with practiced efficiency, and Kade, Mira, Tyra, and Sorin followed the mysterious guide through the shifting sands of the Ashen Desert. The sun began to rise, casting a pale light over the wasteland. The journey was fraught with tension, each step taken with cautious anticipation.

As they traversed the desert, Kade couldn't shake the feeling that they were being watched. The oppressive silence of the wasteland seemed to close in on them, the sands whispering secrets that eluded their understanding. The rider led them with an unerring sense of direction, as if the desert itself was guiding their path.

Hours passed, and the Oasis of the Fallen finally came into view. It was a small, verdant spot amidst the barren wasteland—a stark contrast to the desolation surrounding it. Palm trees and lush greenery encircled a shimmering pool of water, its surface reflecting the harsh sunlight.

Kade felt a surge of relief as they approached the oasis. The guide halted at the edge of the oasis and turned to face them.

"This is where I leave you," the rider said. "Be cautious. The desert is not done with you yet."

Without another word, the rider turned their horse and rode back into the desert's depths, disappearing from sight.

Kade and his companions approached the oasis, the sight of water a welcome relief. They drank deeply, their throats parched from the desert's heat. As they rested by the pool, Kade's thoughts returned to the prophecy and the trials ahead. The oasis offered a brief respite, but the true challenge lay in what awaited them beyond this temporary sanctuary.

The desert had tested their resolve, and Kade knew that the trials were far from over. With a renewed sense of purpose, he led the group in preparing for the next leg of their journey. The wasteland had revealed its harshness, but it had also brought them closer to the truth of their quest. As they set out once more, the desert's trials lingered in their minds, a reminder of the challenges that lay ahead.

The sun hung low in the sky, casting a haunting orange glow over the desolate wasteland. The Ashen Desert stretched endlessly before Kade and his companions, an expanse of withered earth and jagged stone that bore the scars of ancient conflicts. The air was thick with the acrid smell of sulfur and charred remnants, a constant reminder of the cataclysmic battles that had ravaged this land.

Kade trudged forward, his heavy boots kicking up small clouds of ash with each step. His thoughts were consumed by Tyra's recent revelations. The young thief had been more subdued than usual, her eyes distant as though she were peering into another realm. Her visions were becoming more frequent and intense, and Kade's growing concern was mirrored in the furrowed brows of his companions.

The group had made camp for the night in the shadow of a crumbling stone edifice that jutted out of the desert like a skeletal finger pointing to the heavens. As the last light of day faded, the temperature dropped sharply, leaving the desert's surface as cold and unforgiving as the stone.

Tyra sat apart from the others, her eyes closed in concentration. Mira, the mage with her enigmatic aura, was seated nearby, her staff resting against her shoulder as she watched the girl with a mixture of curiosity and apprehension. Sorin, the stoic mercenary, kept a wary eye on their surroundings, his hand never straying far from his weapon.

Kade approached Tyra cautiously, sensing the weight of her visions pressing upon her. "Tyra," he said softly, "what do you see?"

Her eyes fluttered open, revealing the turmoil within. "The Crown," she murmured, her voice trembling. "I've seen it... but it's not as we hoped."

Kade's heart sank. "What do you mean?"

Tyra struggled to articulate her vision. "In my dreams, the Crown is already corrupted. It's surrounded by darkness, and the sky is filled with fire. The gods... they're not coming back. Instead, the Crown is... releasing something."

Mira's expression grew more troubled. "The Crown was supposed to be a key, but if Tyra's visions are correct, it might not be a beacon of salvation at all."

Sorin's eyes narrowed. "If the Crown is corrupted, we might be dealing with something far worse than we imagined. We need to know more."

Kade nodded, though his mind was already racing ahead. "We must find more information. There might be something in the ruins of the old temples here that can shed light on what we face."

As the companions settled for the night, Kade's thoughts were consumed by Tyra's words. He lay awake, staring at the stars hidden behind the veil of smoke and ash. The desolation of the desert seemed to mirror the emptiness he felt inside. He was haunted by the knowledge of his own betrayal, and now it seemed the very relic he sought might bring about the end he had tried to prevent.

The following morning, they resumed their journey, the desert landscape a monotonous sea of gray and brown. The heat was relentless, pressing down on them like an invisible weight. They moved cautiously, the ruins they sought buried somewhere beneath the sands.

After hours of trudging through the wasteland, they came upon a cluster of crumbling stone pillars jutting from the ground. The pillars were remnants of an ancient structure, long forgotten and half-buried in the shifting sands. Kade approached the ruins, his eyes scanning the desolate landscape for any sign of the answers they sought.

Mira stepped forward, her staff glowing faintly as she chanted an incantation. The air around them shimmered, and an ethereal light revealed faint inscriptions on the pillars. "These markings are ancient," she said, her voice reverent. "They speak of a prophecy, one that might be linked to the Crown."

Kade examined the inscriptions, his brow furrowed in concentration. The symbols were unfamiliar, a language lost to time. "Can you translate them?" he asked.

Mira nodded. "It will take time. But there might be clues here about the true nature of the Crown."

As Mira worked on deciphering the inscriptions, Tyra wandered off, her gaze distant. She was drawn to a partially buried altar, its surface etched with more symbols. She knelt beside it, her fingers brushing the dust away. A feeling of unease settled over her as she traced the ancient runes.

Sorin kept a watchful eye on their surroundings, his senses attuned to any potential threats. The desolation of the desert made him nervous, the silence broken only by the occasional gust of wind. "We should be cautious," he said. "This place feels... wrong."

Mira's voice broke through the tension. "I've found something. It's a prophecy about the Crown and its true purpose. It says that the Crown will bring about the end of the world if it is not used correctly."

Kade's heart raced. "What does it say about how to use it correctly?"

Mira hesitated. "It doesn't provide a clear answer. It speaks of a trial, a test of purity, and the need for great sacrifice."

Kade's mind was a whirlwind of thoughts. If the Crown was indeed a harbinger of doom, they had to act quickly. But what did the prophecy mean by a test of purity and sacrifice? The answers were elusive, and the burden of their quest weighed heavily on him.

As the sun dipped below the horizon, casting long shadows over the ruins, Kade and his companions gathered around the campfire. The heat of the day had given way to a cold, biting wind. They sat in silence, each lost in their own thoughts.

Tyra spoke up, her voice trembling. "I've had another vision. The Crown is not just an object. It's a key to something much older, something that was locked away by the gods. If we fail, it will be unleashed."

Mira looked at Tyra with concern. "Do you know what it is?"

Tyra shook her head. "I don't know, but I feel it's tied to the darkness that has plagued this land for centuries."

The gravity of their situation was sinking in. The Crown was not the salvation they had hoped for but a potential catalyst for the world's destruction. Kade's resolve hardened. They needed to find out everything they could about the ancient evil before it was too late.

As they prepared to rest for the night, Kade's mind was filled with a growing sense of urgency. The journey ahead would be fraught with danger, and the path to the Crown was shrouded in uncertainty. But one thing was clear: the fate of the world rested on their shoulders, and they could not afford to fail.

The desert night was cold and silent, broken only by the whispers of the wind. The companions lay in their makeshift camp, each lost in their own thoughts, as the ancient ruins around them seemed to hold their secrets close. The trials ahead would test their resolve, and the darkness that lay ahead was more daunting than any of them could have anticipated.

Chapter 6: The Forgotten Prophecy

The Ashen Desert stretched before them like a sea of rusted gold, shimmering under the harsh midday sun. The air was a heavy, oppressive blanket, suffused with the stench of burnt earth and the echoes of ancient wars. Kade and his companions trudged through the desolate expanse, their movements sluggish under the weight of their exhaustion. Every step seemed to pull them deeper into the heart of the wasteland, where the remnants of forgotten battles lay buried beneath layers of ash.

The desert's relentless heat was only matched by the scorching intensity of their doubts. Tyra's revelations from the previous night had unsettled them all. Her dreams, once dismissed as mere figments of an overactive imagination, now seemed to hold a deeper significance. If her visions of the Crown were to be believed, they were racing against a clock, with each passing moment adding to the corruption that had already tainted the relic.

Mira, ever vigilant, scanned the horizon with her sharp eyes. Her magical senses were on high alert, searching for any sign of danger or the hidden oracle that was rumored to dwell in these arid plains. Her silence was a testament to her concentration; she was attempting to piece together the fragments of the prophecy she had heard long ago.

Sorin, the mercenary, was less reserved in his demeanor. He grumbled under his breath, the heat and the endless stretch of sand testing his patience. "Are we sure this is the right way?" he asked for the umpteenth time. "This wasteland feels endless. And I don't like the idea of stumbling into an oracle that might just be a mirage."

Kade, his face lined with both exhaustion and a deep-seated worry, glanced at Sorin. "The visions Tyra had showed the Crown already corrupted. We need answers, and the oracle is our best hope."

Tyra, leading the group, had taken to mumbling softly to herself, her brows furrowed in concentration. Her dreams had been vivid and disturbing, depicting a Crown tainted by an otherworldly darkness. She had seen images of twisted landscapes and shadowy figures, and the more she tried to recall, the more fragmented the visions became.

The sun dipped lower in the sky, casting long shadows across the sand. Just as the group began to lose hope, Mira's sharp eyes caught sight of an unusual formation on the horizon—a cluster of ancient, crumbling spires that seemed to rise from the desert floor like the skeletal remains of a long-forgotten civilization.

"Over there," Mira pointed, her voice cutting through the silence. "Those spires might be a sign of the oracle's domain."

As they approached the spires, the temperature dropped abruptly. A sudden, chilling breeze swept through the area, carrying with it a sense of foreboding. The spires, now clearly ancient ruins, were etched with faded runes that glowed faintly in the dying light.

The group entered the ruins, their footsteps echoing off the stone walls. The air was cooler inside, a welcome relief from the oppressive heat of the desert. The walls were adorned with ancient symbols and murals depicting battles between gods and monstrous entities.

In the heart of the ruins, they found the oracle—a figure draped in tattered robes, seated upon a stone altar. Her eyes, though old and clouded, held a sharpness that belied her age. She was surrounded by artifacts and relics of a bygone era, and a faint, eerie light seemed to emanate from her.

The oracle looked up as they approached, her gaze lingering on each of them with a penetrating intensity. "You have come seeking answers," she said, her voice a raspy whisper that seemed to echo through the chamber. "But be warned, the truth you seek may come at a great cost."

Kade stepped forward, his heart pounding with a mixture of hope and dread. "We need to know about the Crown of the Fallen," he said. "What is its true purpose?"

The oracle's gaze settled on Kade, her expression one of deep contemplation. "The Crown is not merely a relic of the gods but a harbinger of doom. It was created to bind the ancient evil, not to resurrect the gods."

Mira's eyes widened. "Bind? You mean to imprison?"

"Yes," the oracle replied. "The gods' fall was not an accident; it was a deliberate act to protect the world from an entity older than time itself. The Crown was the key to its imprisonment, not its resurrection."

Kade's mind raced. The weight of his past sins seemed to press down on him more heavily than ever. "But why was the Crown stolen? And how does it fit with the prophecy Tyra has seen?"

The oracle's eyes flickered to Tyra, who was now clutching her amulet tightly. "The prophecy speaks of a great evil that will rise when the Crown is used. Tyra's dreams are echoes of this prophecy. The Crown, once corrupted, will not restore the gods but will release the darkness it was meant to contain."

Tyra's face was pale, and she looked at Kade with a mixture of fear and determination. "So, the visions I've had... they were warnings, not just dreams. The Crown is already corrupted, and it's only a matter of time before it's fully unleashed."

Kade felt a cold sweat break out on his brow. The reality of their situation was becoming more dire with each passing moment. "What must we do?" he asked, desperation creeping into his voice. "How can we prevent this catastrophe?"

The oracle's gaze softened, and she leaned forward. "To prevent the release of the ancient evil, you must destroy the Crown. But be warned, its destruction will come with a heavy price. The very essence of the evil it contains will seek to escape, and it will test your resolve and your souls."

Sorin, ever pragmatic, spoke up. "And what of the prophecy? What happens to us if we destroy the Crown?"

"The prophecy speaks of the end of one era and the beginning of another," the oracle said. "The world will change, and those who seek to protect it will be tested in ways they cannot yet comprehend. The Crown's destruction will be the catalyst for this change."

The gravity of the oracle's words settled over them like a shroud. Kade could see the uncertainty in the eyes of his companions, each grappling with the enormity of their task. The journey ahead would not only be perilous but fraught with personal trials.

The oracle's gaze turned back to Kade. "You carry the burden of the gods' fall and the ancient evil. Your choices will determine the fate of the world. Remember, redemption is not given but earned through sacrifice and courage."

With those final words, the oracle closed her eyes and fell silent. The group stood in the dim light of the chamber, their minds reeling from the revelations. The path ahead was now clearer but infinitely more daunting.

Kade took a deep breath, steeling himself for the trials to come. The weight of his past sins, the responsibility for his daughter's fate, and the impending danger of the ancient evil all pressed heavily upon him. Yet, with newfound determination, he knew that their quest was far from over.

As they prepared to leave the ruins and face the challenges that lay ahead, Kade resolved to lead his companions with the strength and wisdom that the oracle's prophecy demanded. The fate of the world rested on their shoulders, and they could not afford to falter now.

Kade's mind reeled from the oracle's revelation. The words of the prophecy echoed in his ears, a haunting melody of doom and destruction. The Crown, which had been their beacon of hope, was now a harbinger of calamity. The weight of this newfound knowledge pressed down on him, threatening to crush his resolve.

The oracle's cavern, hidden deep within the wasteland, was a place of eerie stillness, the air thick with ancient power. The flickering torchlight cast long shadows against the stone walls, creating an illusion of movement where there was none. Mira, Tyra, and Sorin stood around Kade, their faces illuminated by the trembling flames.

"The prophecy speaks of an ancient evil," Mira said softly, her voice barely above a whisper. "But what exactly is this evil? And why does it tie so closely to you, Kade?"

Kade looked at Mira, his eyes darkened with a mixture of fear and determination. "The oracle's words were clear. The Crown is not a tool of salvation but a key to unlocking something far worse than we can imagine. This evil was bound by the gods themselves, and now it seems that the Crown is the only way to set it free."

Tyra, standing off to the side, shivered despite the oppressive heat of the wasteland. "I've seen the Crown in my dreams, as I've told you before. But now... now I fear that my dreams were a glimpse of something far more terrifying. What if the Crown isn't just a key, but also a part of the evil itself?"

Sorin, who had been silent throughout the exchange, finally spoke up. His voice was gruff, but there was an edge of concern in it. "We need more than just prophecies and dreams to understand this. We need facts, a plan. The wasteland is no place for idle speculation."

The group fell into a tense silence, each member grappling with the gravity of their situation. Kade's gaze drifted to the oracle, who sat cross-legged on a stone dais, her eyes closed as if in deep meditation. Her presence seemed almost otherworldly, a living relic from a forgotten age.

The oracle finally spoke, her voice a mere whisper that seemed to resonate with the very essence of the cavern. "The truth you seek lies not just in the Crown but in the blood that binds you to the ancient evil. Kade, you are not merely a pawn in this game. You are part of a lineage that has been cursed and blessed with the very power that the gods sought to contain."

Kade's heart pounded in his chest. "What do you mean? How am I connected to this ancient evil?"

The oracle's eyes fluttered open, revealing depths of knowledge and sorrow. "Your bloodline was once guardians of the gods' secrets. When the betrayal occurred, it was not just the gods who were forsaken. Your ancestors, too, were marked by this evil. You, Kade, are the last of this line. The power of the Crown calls to you because of this connection."

Mira stepped closer to Kade, her face a mask of concern. "You've been carrying this burden all along. Your quest for redemption was not just about recovering the Crown but confronting your own past."

Kade swallowed hard, feeling the weight of the oracle's words. "And what of my daughter? What does she have to do with this?"

The oracle's gaze softened, a trace of sadness evident in her eyes. "Your daughter is not merely a victim of this curse. She is the vessel through which the ancient evil seeks to return. Her blood carries the key to unlocking the power that was bound by the gods. You must choose between her life and the fate of the world."

Kade's knees felt weak, and he sank to the ground, overwhelmed by the burden of the revelation. The prophecy had stripped away any semblance of hope he had clung to.

His mission, once clear and noble, now seemed tainted by the inevitability of despair.

Tyra, who had been silent, spoke with a tremor in her voice. "We need to understand what this evil is and how it can be stopped. If the Crown is the key to releasing it, then we must find a way to either destroy the Crown or contain the evil without sacrificing Kade's daughter."

Sorin nodded in agreement. "Our journey has led us this far. We cannot falter now. We need to find out more about this evil and how it can be stopped. The prophecy might hold more clues, and there might be ancient texts or artifacts that can help us."

Kade looked at his companions, their faces etched with determination. Despite the crushing weight of the prophecy, he could see that they were resolute in their support. They were not just companions but allies bound by a shared mission.

"Very well," Kade said, his voice steadying. "We will continue our quest. We need to find more information about the ancient evil and the role the Crown plays in its release. We cannot let this curse define our fate. If there is a chance to save my daughter and the world, we must take it."

The oracle's expression was one of both approval and sadness. "Your journey will be fraught with peril. The path to understanding and confronting the ancient evil will be long and difficult. But remember, the true power lies not just in the Crown or the evil it might release, but in your choices and the strength of your resolve."

As Kade and his companions prepared to leave the oracle's cavern, the gravity of their situation weighed heavily on them. The wasteland stretched out before them, an expanse of desolation that seemed to mirror their inner turmoil. The prophecy had revealed the harsh truth, but it had also given them a renewed sense of purpose.

The journey ahead would be fraught with danger and uncertainty. The Crown's true nature was a threat to all they held dear, and the choice between saving Kade's daughter or allowing the ancient evil to rise loomed over them like a dark cloud. But for now, they had to focus on the immediate challenge: finding the information they needed to confront the darkness and protect the world from the ancient evil that awaited its release.

As the group made their way out of the cavern and back into the wasteland, each member grappled with their own fears and uncertainties. The road ahead was unknown, and the weight of the prophecy was a constant reminder of the stakes they faced. Yet, united by their shared mission, they pressed forward, determined to unravel the mysteries that lay ahead and confront the darkness that threatened to consume them all.

The sun dipped below the horizon, casting long shadows across the wasteland as Kade and his companions embarked on the next leg of their journey. The ancient evil was a looming threat, and the Crown was the key to its release. With the prophecy guiding them and their resolve unwavering, they ventured forth into the unknown, ready to face whatever challenges awaited them in their quest to save the world from the impending doom.

Chapter 7: The Siege of Blackstone Keep

The journey from the Ashen Desert to Blackstone Keep was fraught with both physical and emotional exhaustion. Kade's group had traversed the vast wasteland, braving the searing heat and the haunting whispers of their past. As the looming silhouette of Blackstone Keep emerged on the horizon, the weight of their quest pressed heavily on their shoulders.

Blackstone Keep was a formidable structure, its stone walls battered by countless sieges and its towers crumbling under the weight of time. Once a proud bastion of the kingdom's might, it now stood as a silent sentinel over a land ravaged by strife. The Keep's presence loomed ominously against the backdrop of a storm-laden sky, foretelling the conflict that was about to erupt.

As the group approached the Keep, the sound of clashing steel and the distant echoes of battle reached their ears. The air was thick with smoke and the acrid scent of burning wood. Kade and his companions quickened their pace, driven by the urgency of their mission and the growing realization that they were racing against time.

"We need to find a way in," Kade urged, his voice barely audible over the din of war. "The Crown won't wait for us."

Mira, her eyes scanning the horizon, spotted a narrow, winding path leading up to the Keep's western gate. "There," she pointed, "we can slip in through there."

Tyra, her nimble frame darting ahead, led the way up the precarious path. Sorin, his face grim, followed closely, his hand resting on the hilt of his sword. Kade, burdened by the weight of his past and the Crown's growing influence, struggled to focus on the task at hand. His mind was a storm of conflicting thoughts and fears, and he could feel the Crown's malevolent pull growing stronger with each step.

As they reached the top of the path, they found themselves overlooking the chaotic battlefield. The Keep's defenders, a ragtag force of soldiers and mercenaries, fought desperately against a rival warlord's army. The ground was littered with fallen warriors, and the clash of weapons rang out like the discordant notes of a symphony of chaos.

Kade's heart sank as he observed the scene. The Keep, their supposed sanctuary and the potential location of the Crown, was now a battleground. The very structure they sought to infiltrate was caught in the throes of a brutal siege.

"We need to get inside," Mira said urgently. "The longer we wait, the harder it will be."

The group descended cautiously, avoiding the main gate where the fighting was fiercest. They managed to find a side entrance partially concealed by debris. As they slipped through, the interior of the Keep revealed a different sort of chaos—rooms overturned, shelves emptied, and the remnants of a once-grand structure now reduced to a shell of its former glory.

The Keep's inner sanctum was eerily quiet, the sounds of battle muffled by thick stone walls. Kade led the way, his steps heavy with the burden of his past actions. His guilt and the Crown's corrupting influence loomed over him like a dark cloud, clouding his judgment and intensifying his sense of urgency.

As they navigated the darkened halls, Mira suddenly halted. "Wait," she whispered, holding up her hand. Her eyes, glowing faintly with arcane light, scanned the area ahead. "Something's not right."

Sorin, ever vigilant, drew his sword. "What do you mean?"

"Magic," Mira said, her voice laced with tension. "I can feel it."

The group pressed forward cautiously, their senses on high alert. As they turned a corner, they were confronted by a sudden surge of magical energy. A shimmering barrier of arcane force materialized before them, blocking their path.

"This is a ward," Mira said, her voice strained. "It's designed to keep intruders out."

Kade's frustration boiled over. "We don't have time for this! We need to find the Crown before it's too late."

Mira approached the barrier, her hands weaving intricate patterns in the air. "If I can disrupt the ward, we can get through."

With a burst of intense energy, Mira's magic collided with the barrier. The ward flickered and wavered but held firm. Mira's face grew pale with exertion, but she continued her efforts, determined to breach the barrier.

As Mira fought against the ward, Tyra's sharp eyes caught movement from the corner of the hallway. A shadowy figure, clad in dark armor, slipped past them and vanished into the depths of the Keep.

"Did anyone else see that?" Tyra asked, her voice tinged with concern.

Kade, his gaze fixed on Mira's struggle, barely acknowledged the question. His mind was consumed by the urgency of their mission and the increasing pressure from the Crown. He could feel its power resonating with a dark energy, a constant reminder of the burden he carried.

Finally, with a flash of brilliance, Mira's spell shattered the barrier. The ward dissipated, leaving the path open. The group pressed on, their footsteps echoing through the desolate halls.

They ventured deeper into the Keep, their progress marked by the wreckage of previous battles. The structure's once-grand halls were now strewn with debris and littered with the remnants of a desperate defense. It was clear that the Keep had been under siege for some time, and its defenders were struggling to hold their ground.

Kade's thoughts were a turbulent mix of past regrets and present fears. The Crown's influence grew stronger with each step, and he could sense its corrupting power seeping into his very being. His mind was plagued by visions of the ancient evil and the terrible choices that awaited him.

As they reached the central chamber of the Keep, Kade's heart sank. The room was a vast, empty space, its stone walls adorned with faded tapestries and broken statues. In the center of the room stood a massive stone pedestal, upon which rested an ornate chest covered in ancient runes.

The chest was bound with heavy chains and locked with a complex mechanism. Kade's eyes were drawn to it, the Crown's influence amplifying his desire to claim it. His hands trembled as he approached the pedestal, and his companions watched in tense silence.

Mira, still recovering from her previous efforts, examined the chest with a mixture of awe and apprehension. "This is it," she said softly. "The Crown must be inside."

Tyra, her gaze flickering between Kade and the chest, voiced her concerns. "We need to be careful. There could be traps."

Kade nodded, his mind focused on the task at hand. He moved to unlock the chest, his hands working with practiced precision. The mechanism clicked open, revealing a richly decorated interior.

But as the lid of the chest creaked open, a deafening roar echoed through the Keep. The walls trembled, and the very ground seemed to shake. Kade and his companions were thrown off balance as the sound of the siege intensified.

In the midst of the chaos, a figure emerged from the shadows—a man clad in dark, ornate armor, his face obscured by a horned helmet. He moved with an air of authority, his presence commanding immediate attention.

Kade's heart raced as the figure approached, his eyes gleaming with a cold, calculating gaze. The man's armor bore the insignia of the rival warlord who had laid siege to the Keep. It was clear that the warlord's forces were closing in, and the final confrontation was imminent.

The figure raised his hand, and a surge of dark magic burst forth, engulfing the central chamber in a swirling vortex of energy. Kade and his companions were thrown to the floor, their vision obscured by the powerful magic.

Through the haze, Kade could see the warlord's forces converging on the Keep. The final battle was about to begin, and the fate of their quest hung in the balance.

With a sense of grim determination, Kade rose to his feet, his gaze fixed on the pedestal and the Crown within. He knew that their mission was far from over and that the coming battle would test their resolve and their unity.

As the roar of battle grew louder, Kade and his companions prepared to face the ultimate challenge. The siege of Blackstone Keep was about to reach its climax, and the stakes had never been higher.

The clang of steel on steel resonated through the air as the siege of Blackstone Keep continued unabated. The roar of battle seemed endless, a brutal symphony that drowned out all other sounds. Kade and his companions fought their way through the tumultuous chaos of the battlefield, desperate to find a way to reach the inner sanctum of the keep where the Crown was rumored to be hidden.

Kade, his armor battered and smeared with blood, barely registered the struggle around him. His focus was singular: the keep's towering walls and the darkened entrance that might lead them to the Crown. His mind raced as he thought about the consequences of the battle. The struggle was not just for survival but for the Crown—a relic that could decide the fate of the entire world. Mira and Tyra fought alongside him, their skills complementing each other in a desperate bid to push through the enemy ranks.

Mira's magic flared like a beacon in the storm of combat, her spells weaving through the battlefield with precision. Each wave of energy she released created a temporary haven amidst the chaos, buying them precious moments to advance. Her eyes, usually so calm, were now steely with determination as she cast barrier after barrier to protect them from the relentless onslaught.

Tyra, though young and seemingly fragile, moved with an agility that belied her appearance. Her small frame darted through the throng of fighters, slipping past enemies and striking with deadly accuracy. Her instincts guided her as she collected vital information from overheard conversations, relaying it back to Kade with urgency.

As they fought, Kade's thoughts were interrupted by a sudden, piercing cry. Mira's voice cut through the clamor, filled with fear. "Kade, they've taken Mira!" she shouted, her words barely audible over the din of the battle.

Kade's heart sank. Mira had been a crucial part of their journey, and her capture could turn the tide of the conflict against them. He glanced toward the keep, where Mira had been separated from them in the chaos. Her absence left a gaping hole in their ranks, and Kade knew that they could not afford to lose her.

Struggling against the tide of enemies, Kade and Tyra fought their way towards the keep's entrance. Every step felt like a mile as they pushed through the fray, each encounter with an enemy soldier more harrowing than the last. The gates of Blackstone Keep loomed closer, but so did the realization that time was running out. They had to secure the Crown before it was too late, and now, without Mira's magic to shield them, their chances seemed bleak.

As they neared the keep's entrance, Kade spotted the warlord leading the siege—a man known only as Roderic, feared for his ruthless tactics and formidable strength. Kade had never met Roderic, but the warlord's reputation preceded him. The man's imposing figure was a dark silhouette against the flames of the burning keep, his presence a constant reminder of the dire circumstances they faced.

Kade and Tyra fought their way to Roderic's command tent, where the warlord appeared to be directing the siege. The tent was a rare moment of relative calm amidst the chaos, and Kade seized the opportunity to confront Roderic. Bursting into the tent, Kade saw the warlord seated at a table, maps spread out before him, a look of grim satisfaction on his face as he observed the battle's progress.

Roderic looked up, his eyes narrowing as he took in the sight of Kade. "You're the one who's been making trouble for me," Roderic said, his voice a low growl. "What do you want?"

Kade did not hesitate. "Mira has been captured," he said, his voice edged with desperation. "We need her back. And we need access to the keep's inner chambers."

Roderic's expression remained unreadable as he considered Kade's plea. "Why should I help you?" he asked, leaning back in his chair. "What's in it for me?"

Kade's mind raced. He knew he had little to offer in return, but he had to find a way to secure Roderic's cooperation. "The Crown of the Fallen," Kade said finally. "I can lead you to it. Help me rescue Mira, and I'll take you to the Crown. It's hidden within the keep."

Roderic's eyes glinted with interest. "The Crown, you say? If you're telling the truth, then we might have a deal." He stood up, his large frame casting a shadow over the room. "But first, you'll need to prove your worth. I want the keep's gatehouse secured and the enemy forces repelled. Only then will I consider helping you."

The terms were harsh, but Kade had no choice. He nodded grimly. "Agreed."

Kade and Tyra returned to the fray, determined to meet Roderic's demands. They fought their way to the gatehouse, where they encountered fierce resistance from the enemy forces. The battle for control of the gatehouse was brutal, but Kade's determination never wavered. With Tyra's support, they managed to drive back the attackers and secure the gatehouse, allowing Roderic's forces to gain a crucial advantage.

Exhausted but victorious, Kade returned to Roderic's tent to report their success. Roderic was waiting for him, a glimmer of approval in his eyes. "You've done well," Roderic said. "Now, I'll honor my end of the bargain. But remember, once we've secured the Crown, our alliance ends. I have my own plans for the relic."

With a curt nod, Kade agreed. He and Tyra were led by Roderic's men through the keep's inner defenses, making their way to the chambers where Mira was being held. The path was treacherous, filled with traps and ambushes, but Kade's resolve was unwavering.

Finally, they reached the cell where Mira was imprisoned. She looked up as the door was opened, her face pale but her spirit unbroken. Relief washed over her as she saw Kade and

Tyra. "I knew you'd come," she said, her voice hoarse but determined.

Kade quickly unlocked her cell, and Mira stepped out, her eyes scanning the surroundings. "We need to move quickly," she said. "The warlord's men are still searching for the Crown, and we have to reach it before they do."

With Mira safely back in their company, the group pushed forward towards the keep's inner sanctum. The tension was palpable as they navigated the labyrinthine corridors of the keep, each step bringing them closer to their goal.

As they reached the final chamber where the Crown was said to be hidden, Kade's heart raced. The door was adorned with ancient runes, a testament to the relic's power. With a deep breath, Kade pushed open the door, revealing a chamber bathed in a dim, eerie light.

In the center of the chamber stood a pedestal, and on it rested the Crown of the Fallen. The relic was even more magnificent than Kade had imagined, its surface etched with intricate designs that seemed to shift and change in the flickering light.

But before they could approach the Crown, a chilling realization struck Kade. The air around them grew colder, and a shadowy figure emerged from the darkness, its form shifting and indistinct. The figure's presence was malevolent, a reminder of the ancient evil that Kade had hoped to avoid.

Mira's eyes widened as she recognized the figure. "We're not alone," she warned. "Something is guarding the Crown."

The figure advanced slowly, its presence a dark cloud that seemed to sap the light from the chamber. Kade felt a shiver run down his spine as he prepared to face the guardian of the Crown. The final confrontation was at hand, and the fate of their quest—and perhaps the world itself—hung in the balance.

As the guardian drew closer, Kade steeled himself for the battle to come. The relic was within reach, but obtaining it would require more than just strength and skill. It would take every ounce of courage and resolve Kade possessed, for the true test was only beginning.

Chapter 8: The Heart of the Keep

The battle for Blackstone Keep had left the castle in ruins, its once-proud walls now marred by the scars of war. As the final echoes of the conflict faded into a tense silence, Kade, Mira, and Sorin surveyed the damage from the safety of the keep's main hall. The structure groaned under the weight of destruction, its grand archways and vaulted ceilings reduced to shattered stone and twisted metal.

Kade's eyes were fixed on the narrow staircase leading down into the heart of the keep. The Crown of the Fallen was rumored to be hidden deep within the ancient tunnels beneath the castle, and their path was clear, though fraught with peril. He turned to Mira, whose expression was a mix of exhaustion and determination.

"Are you ready?" Kade asked, his voice betraying his own fatigue. His once-pristine armor was now dented and smeared with grime. The weight of his guilt seemed to press harder on his shoulders with each passing moment.

Mira, adjusting her robes and brushing off dust, gave him a nod. "We don't have much time. The Crown is not going to wait for us to recover."

Sorin, ever the pragmatist, was already examining their dwindling supplies. "We need to be cautious. There are likely traps and guardians. Blackstone Keep has its own defenses, and we've already seen what's lurking in these ruins."

The trio descended into the depths of the keep, the flickering torches casting long shadows on the stone walls. The staircase was steep and narrow, twisting down into the darkness. Each step echoed eerily, a reminder of the silence that had descended after the chaos.

As they reached the base of the stairs, they entered a large underground chamber. The air was damp and cool, a stark contrast to the heat of the battle above. The chamber was dimly lit by bioluminescent fungi growing on the walls, casting an eerie, greenish glow. Ancient murals depicting gods and mythical creatures adorned the walls, their colors faded but still vibrant enough to evoke a sense of reverence.

In the center of the chamber stood a large stone door, covered in intricate carvings. It was adorned with symbols and runes that pulsed faintly with a bluish light. Kade approached the door, his heart racing. This was the entrance to the final leg of their journey.

"This is it," Kade said, running his hand over the carvings. "The Crown should be beyond this door."

Mira stepped forward, her staff glowing with magical energy. "I can sense powerful wards and enchantments protecting this place. We'll need to be careful."

Kade nodded, feeling a mix of anticipation and dread. The journey had been fraught with danger, and this final stretch promised to be no different. He glanced at Sorin, who was examining the door's mechanism with practiced eyes.

"Any advice for us?" Kade asked.

Sorin's face was grim. "We need to move quickly. The warlord's forces will eventually make their way down here, and if we're not careful, we could find ourselves in a much worse situation."

With a deep breath, Mira began to cast a spell, her voice a low murmur as she chanted the incantation. The runes on the door glowed brighter, and the door creaked open, revealing a dark passage beyond.

The air was thick with the smell of decay and ancient magic. As Kade, Mira, and Sorin stepped through the doorway, they entered a long, narrow tunnel. The walls were lined with old carvings and ancient scripts, telling stories of battles long forgotten and gods long abandoned. The passage seemed to stretch endlessly, a labyrinth of forgotten history.

They moved cautiously, their footsteps echoing off the stone walls. The deeper they ventured, the more oppressive the atmosphere became. The tunnel was cold and damp, and every now and then, they could hear the faintest sound of something scurrying in the darkness.

"Stay alert," Kade instructed. "We don't know what could be waiting for us."

The tunnel finally opened into a vast underground chamber. It was massive, with a high, vaulted ceiling supported by ancient pillars. The air was colder here, and a faint mist clung to the ground, swirling around their feet.

In the center of the chamber was an elaborate pedestal, upon which rested a large, ornate chest. The chest was covered in intricate runes and symbols, and its surface gleamed with a faint, golden light.

"There it is," Mira whispered, her eyes fixed on the chest. "The Crown must be inside."

Kade approached the pedestal, his heart pounding in his chest. The room was eerily silent, the only sound being the distant drip of water from the ceiling. He could feel the weight of centuries pressing down on him as he reached out to open the chest.

Before he could touch it, however, the chamber was suddenly filled with a chilling, guttural growl. From the shadows emerged a horde of nightmarish creatures—twisted, skeletal beings with glowing red eyes and razor-sharp claws. They seemed to materialize out of the very darkness itself, their presence a testament to the ancient evils that lurked within the keep.

Kade drew his sword, Mira readied her staff, and Sorin brandished his blades. The creatures advanced with a menacing speed, their growls growing louder and more frenzied.

"Fight them off!" Kade shouted. "We need to secure the Crown!"

The battle was fierce and unrelenting. Kade and Sorin fought valiantly, their blades flashing in the dim light as they cut down the grotesque creatures. Mira, her staff crackling with magical energy, unleashed powerful spells that sent bursts of light through the chamber, driving the creatures back.

Despite their best efforts, the horde seemed endless. For every creature they felled, more seemed to appear from the shadows. The chamber became a chaotic melee, a swirling vortex of violence and desperation.

Amidst the chaos, Kade's focus remained on the pedestal. He could see the faint glimmer of the Crown through the open chest, tantalizingly close. He fought his way through the creatures, determined to reach it.

As he reached the pedestal, a massive creature—a grotesque amalgamation of bone and shadow—stepped forward, its eyes glowing with an unnatural intelligence. It let out a deafening roar and charged at Kade with terrifying force.

Kade braced himself, his sword poised to strike. The creature lunged, its claws slashing through the air. Kade met its attack with a powerful swing of his blade, but the creature was incredibly strong and fast. They engaged in a brutal clash, the creature's claws raking across Kade's armor as he parried and countered with all his might.

Finally, with a desperate thrust, Kade drove his sword into the creature's heart. It let out a final, blood-curdling scream before collapsing into a pile of dust and shadow. The chamber fell silent once more.

Kade, breathing heavily, approached the chest. The lid was slightly ajar, revealing the Crown of the Fallen nestled inside. He reached in and carefully lifted the relic, feeling its weight and the strange, pulsing energy emanating from it.

The Crown was a masterpiece of ancient craftsmanship, made of gold and adorned with precious stones. Its surface was inscribed with runes and symbols that seemed to shift and change as Kade held it.

"We have it," Mira said, her voice a mix of relief and concern. "But we need to leave this place before more of those creatures return."

Kade nodded, his eyes still fixed on the Crown. The power of the relic was palpable, a heavy presence that seemed to press against his very soul. He could feel its ancient magic thrumming with a dark promise, and he knew that their journey was far from over.

As they prepared to leave the chamber, Kade couldn't shake the feeling that their victory had come at a cost. The ancient evil that had been bound within the keep was now awakened, and the Crown's true purpose was yet to be fully revealed.

The path back to the surface was just as treacherous as their descent, but they pressed on, driven by the knowledge that their quest was nearing its climax. The stakes had never been higher, and the true nature of the Crown of the Fallen was still shrouded in mystery.

With the Crown in their possession, Kade, Mira, and Sorin emerged from the depths of Blackstone Keep, their faces set with grim determination. The world outside was still in turmoil, and their journey was far from over. But for now, they had secured a crucial piece of the puzzle, and the next chapter of their quest awaited.

The corridors of Blackstone Keep stretched into darkness, their once-grand architecture now choked by shadows and dust. Kade, Mira, and the remaining members of their group—their ranks thinned by battle and betrayal—navigated the twisting maze beneath the keep, their path lit only by the flickering flames of torches. The ancient relic, the Crown of the Fallen, awaited them in these forsaken depths, guarded by the very nightmares of legend.

As they ventured deeper into the keep's bowels, the oppressive silence was broken only by the faint echoes of their footsteps and the occasional drip of water from the damp stone walls. Kade's heart pounded in his chest, a mix of anticipation and dread. The air grew colder, heavy with an ancient power that seemed to seep from the very stones. Every step he took felt like a step closer to his own doom.

Mira walked beside him, her face pale but determined. Her eyes, normally so full of hidden secrets, were now focused with a steely resolve. She had grown quieter since their last confrontation, as if the weight of their quest had settled heavily upon her shoulders. Tyra, the young thief, and Sorin, the mercenary, flanked their party, each silently bracing themselves for the trials ahead.

"We must be close," Mira murmured, her voice a mere whisper. "The magic here is... overwhelming."

Kade nodded, though his thoughts were consumed by the Crown itself. He had seen its image in old tomes and heard its legends, but nothing could have prepared him for the gravity of this moment. The Crown of the Fallen was said to have been created in the dawn of the gods' reign, a relic imbued with unimaginable power. But what had once been a symbol of divine sovereignty was now a beacon of potential destruction.

They turned a corner and came upon a massive, arched door, its surface adorned with intricate runes that glowed faintly in the torchlight. Kade's breath caught in his throat. This was it—the final barrier between them and the Crown. His hand instinctively reached for the hilt of his sword, but he knew that the true threat lay beyond this door.

Mira stepped forward and began to chant softly, her hands moving in fluid motions as she wove a spell of unlocking. The runes on the door shimmered and pulsed with a soft light, responding to her magic. After a tense moment, the door creaked open, revealing a vast chamber beyond.

The chamber was immense, its ceiling lost in shadow. Massive stone pillars rose from the floor, each one etched with ancient symbols and scenes of celestial battles. At the center of the room stood a pedestal, and upon it rested the Crown of the Fallen. The relic gleamed with a malevolent radiance, its surface shifting like liquid metal.

Kade felt a shiver of both awe and fear as he approached the pedestal. The Crown was as beautiful as it was terrifying, an intricate piece of craftsmanship that seemed to pulse with a life of its own. He reached out to take it, his hand trembling.

A low, guttural growl reverberated through the chamber. The shadows around the pedestal seemed to writhe and twist, coalescing into monstrous shapes. The nightmarish creatures that had guarded the Crown now emerged from the darkness, their eyes glowing with an otherworldly light.

"Prepare yourselves!" Kade shouted, drawing his sword. The others rushed to his side, their weapons ready. Mira's hands flared with magical energy, while Sorin readied his bow.

The creatures lunged at them with feral speed. They were twisted amalgamations of flesh and shadow, their forms shifting and changing as they attacked. Kade swung his sword with precise, practiced movements, each strike accompanied by a burst of divine energy. The creatures recoiled from the holy power, but more seemed to rise from the darkness.

Mira unleashed a torrent of fire from her outstretched hands, her spell illuminating the chamber in a brilliant blaze. The flames seared through the creatures, but their numbers seemed endless. Tyra darted between the combatants, her small blades flashing as she struck at the monsters' vulnerable spots.

As the battle raged, Kade's gaze remained fixed on the Crown. It was tantalizingly close, but the creatures were relentless. Each time he thought they had gained the upper hand, more emerged from the shadows.

Finally, with a surge of strength and determination, Kade pushed through the last of the nightmarish guardians. He reached the pedestal and took the Crown in his hands. The moment he touched it, a jolt of energy surged through him, almost knocking him to his knees. He staggered but managed to hold on to the relic.

A flood of visions overwhelmed him. He saw the ancient evil that the Crown had bound, an entity of incomprehensible darkness that had been imprisoned by the gods. The visions showed its potential to bring ruin to the world, to consume everything in its path.

Gasping, Kade tore his gaze away from the Crown, his mind reeling. The relic's true purpose became horrifyingly clear: it was not a tool for resurrection but a key to releasing the ancient evil. He was holding the very thing that could unleash a catastrophe beyond imagination.

"Quickly!" Mira's voice broke through his daze. "We need to leave before—"

A powerful tremor shook the chamber, and the ground beneath them began to crack. The pedestal shattered, and the ceiling began to collapse. The chamber was crumbling around them.

Kade's heart pounded as he looked around in panic. He clutched the Crown tightly, but his thoughts were consumed by the danger closing in on them. The Crown's power was too great, and they needed to escape before the ancient evil they had inadvertently unleashed could wreak havoc.

"Move!" Kade shouted, leading the way as they fled the collapsing chamber. The echoes of their footsteps were drowned out by the roar of falling debris and the screeching of the shadows. They fought their way through the collapsing tunnels, the weight of their impending doom heavy upon them.

As they emerged into the relative safety of the keep's outer passages, the Crown still clutched in Kade's hand, he felt the full weight of their predicament. They had obtained the relic, but at what cost? The ancient evil was now a step closer to freedom, and the world's fate hung precariously in the balance.

The group regrouped outside the keep, their faces grim and their bodies battered from the fight. Kade looked at Mira, Tyra, and Sorin, their expressions mirroring his own sense of dread.

"We need to get out of here," Kade said, his voice heavy with the burden of what he had learned. "We have to find a way to stop this before it's too late."

Mira nodded, her eyes reflecting the same determination. "We've come too far to turn back now. We need to uncover the truth about the Crown and find a way to prevent the ancient evil from being released."

The journey ahead would be fraught with danger and uncertainty, but Kade knew they had no other choice. The Crown of the Fallen was in their possession, but the true battle was just beginning. With the world at stake, they had to confront the darkness that had been unleashed and find a way to save what remained of their shattered world.

As they prepared to leave the keep and continue their quest, Kade glanced one last time at the crumbling fortress. The echoes of their struggle lingered in the air, a stark reminder of the price they would have to pay for their pursuit of redemption.

The path ahead was fraught with peril, but the stakes had never been higher. With the ancient evil on the brink of being unleashed, Kade and his companions had to push forward, driven by the hope that they could still save their world from the darkness that threatened to consume it.

Chapter 9: Fractured Loyalties

The corridors of Blackstone Keep felt as though they were closing in on Kade. The darkened stone walls, once majestic, now seemed to pulse with the malevolent energy that he had unleashed. Every echo of his footsteps reverberated with the haunting knowledge of what he had found. The Crown of the Fallen, now in his possession, was a weight heavier than any physical burden he had ever known.

The Keep had fallen silent after the battle, the cries of combat replaced by the ominous quiet of aftermath. Kade, Mira, and the few remaining companions—Sorin and Tyra—were the only ones left to navigate this treacherous fortress. The conflict with the warlord had left its scars, and Kade was not merely fighting an external enemy but grappling with the dark forces that were now awakening within him.

The Crown had already begun its insidious work. Kade felt a constant pull, a whispering in his mind that he struggled to ignore. Every vision was a tormenting glimpse into the ancient evil's rise. He had hoped to find answers, but instead, he was mired in confusion and fear. The Crown's true nature was becoming painfully clear; it was not a beacon of salvation but a key to releasing the horrors bound within.

As he moved through the abandoned halls, Mira's warnings echoed in his mind. Her words had been full of dread, yet Kade could not abandon the Crown now. He believed that it was the only way to save the world, even if it meant succumbing to its corrupting influence.

"Do you really think this is worth it?" Mira's voice broke through his reverie. She stood a few paces behind him, her face etched with concern. "The Crown is changing you. It's warping your judgment."

Kade turned to face her, his eyes shadowed by the weight of his burden. "I have to believe it's the key. If we can control it—"

"Control it?" Mira interrupted, her voice rising in frustration. "You don't understand what you're dealing with. The Crown is an artifact of unimaginable power. It's not something you can control, Kade. It's something that controls you."

Sorin, who had been quietly observing, stepped forward. "We need to decide what to do next. The warlord's forces are regrouping, and we can't stay here indefinitely. We also need to address the growing tension within the group. We're fractured, and this division is only going to make things worse."

Kade clenched his fists. He had hoped the Crown would provide answers or at least a clear path forward, but instead, it was driving wedges between them. Trust was eroding as quickly as the Keep's walls were crumbling. He could see it in Sorin's eyes and hear it in Tyra's distant silence.

"Trust me," Kade said finally, his voice heavy with the burden of leadership. "We're close. The Crown's power might be the only way to counter the ancient evil that's awakening. If we let it go now, everything we've fought for will be in vain."

Mira's eyes flashed with anger and desperation. "And if it consumes you? If it turns you into the very evil we're trying to fight? Is that what you want, Kade?"

Her words cut deep, and Kade felt a pang of doubt. The darkness within him seemed to whisper in agreement with Mira's fears. But he pushed the thoughts aside, determined to see their quest through to the end.

They moved through the Keep, their path taking them to the lower levels where the Crown was said to be secured. The air grew colder, the walls slick with dampness, and shadows seemed to stretch and contort with malicious intent. Each step deeper into the abyss was a step further from the light of hope and closer to the heart of the darkness they sought to confront.

The Keep's underground chambers were a labyrinth of ancient stone and forgotten lore. The corridors were lined with the faded symbols of an age long past. The relics of a once-great civilization lay scattered, forgotten by time. Kade's footsteps echoed louder here, as though the very stones were calling out to him, demanding he confront the truth.

"We need to find the chamber where the Crown is kept," Kade said, his voice reverberating through the empty halls.

Mira's expression was tense as she scanned the surroundings. "The legends spoke of a hidden door, but they never mentioned where it was or how to open it. We'll have to rely on the clues we gathered from the siege."

Tyra, who had been unusually quiet, suddenly spoke up. "I have a feeling about this place. It's like... like there's something here that's waiting for us."

Kade looked at her, puzzled by her vague sense of foreboding. "What do you mean?"

Tyra hesitated before speaking. "When I was in the desert, I had a vision. The Crown was shown to me, but it was surrounded by darkness. I think... I think this place is connected to that vision."

Kade's heart sank as he realized the implications of her words. If Tyra's vision was accurate, their search for the Crown might lead them into even greater peril. He glanced at Mira and Sorin, both of whom looked equally concerned.

The group continued their descent, moving through increasingly narrow and treacherous passages. The air was heavy with a sense of foreboding, and every creak and groan of the ancient Keep seemed to echo with the promise of doom. Kade felt the weight of the Crown's power pressing down on him, threatening to overwhelm his senses and cloud his judgment.

Suddenly, they reached a large chamber. The walls were adorned with ancient carvings depicting the gods and their battles with the forces of darkness. In the center of the room was a raised platform, and on it, a large, ornate chest. The Crown of the Fallen was rumored to be within.

Kade approached the chest with a mixture of awe and dread. His heart raced as he reached for the lid, but a sudden tremor shook the chamber. The ground beneath them began to quake, and the ancient symbols on the walls glowed with an eerie light.

"Get back!" Mira shouted, pulling Kade away from the chest. The chamber began to collapse around them, rocks falling from the ceiling and debris scattering across the floor.

Kade and his companions scrambled to escape the collapsing chamber. The once-sturdy walls were giving way, and the passage they had come through was quickly being sealed off by falling debris. They had no choice but to find another way out.

As they fought their way through the crumbling passages, Kade's mind raced with thoughts of the Crown. It was so close, yet now it seemed that fate itself was determined to keep it from them. The tension between the companions was palpable, each one grappling with their fears and doubts as they navigated the perilous labyrinth.

Finally, they emerged into a larger, more stable chamber. Panting and covered in dust, they looked back at the wreckage of the passage they had just escaped. The Crown's chamber was now lost to them, buried beneath the rubble.

Kade was torn between frustration and determination. They had come so far, but the Crown remained just out of reach. The revelations about its true nature were weighing heavily on him, and the fractures within the group were widening.

"Are you okay?" Mira asked, her voice laced with concern.

Kade nodded, though his expression was grim. "We have to regroup and figure out our next move. We can't afford to let this setback destroy us."

The group sat down to catch their breath and plan their next steps. The weight of their quest was pressing down on them, and the fractures within the group were becoming more evident. Trust was eroding, and the tension between Kade and the others was palpable.

As they discussed their options, Kade couldn't shake the feeling that their journey was reaching a critical juncture. The Crown was within their grasp, but the darkness it harbored was beginning to tear them apart. The battle for their unity was as crucial as the battle for the Crown itself.

The path ahead was uncertain, and the cost of their quest was becoming increasingly clear. Kade knew that the real challenge was not just finding the Crown, but overcoming the darkness that was threatening to consume them from within.

With heavy hearts and a sense of impending doom, the companions prepared to continue their quest. The Crown was a beacon of hope and despair, and the road ahead would test their resolve in ways they had never imagined.

The Blackstone Keep was a distant, crumbling silhouette against the horizon, silhouetted by the fiery glow of the setting sun. The echoes of the recent battle still reverberated through the ruins, mingling with the harsh, metallic scent of blood and smoke that lingered in the air. Kade and Mira, now fugitives from both their former allies and the enemies they had fought beside, navigated the treacherous landscape with a renewed sense of urgency. Their flight from Blackstone Keep was marked by tension, mistrust, and the looming threat of what lay ahead.

Kade, burdened by the weight of the Crown and the ominous visions it had provoked, felt a sense of isolation despite Mira's presence. His every step seemed heavier, each breath a struggle against the encroaching darkness that threatened to consume him. The Crown's power had begun to corrupt him, amplifying his fears and doubts. Mira's warnings had become a cacophony in his mind, a constant reminder of the perilous path he tread.

Mira, for her part, remained vigilant. Her mage's senses were attuned to the dangers that lurked in the shadows, her eyes scanning their surroundings with a sharp intensity. She had once admired Kade's strength and resolve, but now she saw the fissures that had formed in his character, the internal struggle that threatened to tear him apart. She could feel the dark influence of the Crown seeping into their every interaction, eroding the trust they had built. The question of whether Kade would be able to resist the Crown's lure was becoming more pressing with each passing moment.

"We need to find shelter," Mira said, her voice cutting through the oppressive silence. "The more distance we put between us and the Keep, the better. We can't afford to be caught by the warlord's forces or our own former allies."

Kade nodded, though his gaze remained distant, clouded by his internal turmoil. The Crown was a beacon of power and peril, and its weight on his shoulders seemed to grow heavier by the day. His mind was a battleground, with the voices of doubt and the relentless whispering of the Crown clashing against his will. The desire to wield the Crown's power to save the world battled with the growing realization that its true nature was far more sinister than he had ever imagined.

Their journey took them through desolate landscapes, over treacherous terrain, and into the heart of a wilderness that seemed to mirror Kade's own fractured state of mind. The silence of the wilderness was punctuated only by the occasional rustling of leaves and the distant call of nocturnal creatures.

The world around them was vast and indifferent, a stark contrast to the chaos they had left behind.

As night fell, they made camp in a secluded glen, hidden from prying eyes. Mira set up wards around their temporary refuge, casting protective spells to ward off any unwanted visitors. Kade, lost in thought, sat apart from the campfire, the Crown resting heavily beside him. The flickering firelight cast long, dancing shadows on the surrounding trees, creating a surreal and unsettling atmosphere.

"Mira," Kade said quietly, his voice rough with fatigue, "what if we're too late? What if the Crown is already corrupting everything it touches?"

Mira looked at him, her expression a mixture of concern and resolve. "The Crown is a powerful artifact, but it's not the only force at play here. We still have a chance to stop whatever is coming. We just need to stay focused and not let the Crown's influence cloud our judgment."

Kade nodded, though his expression remained troubled. He knew Mira was right, but the weight of the Crown and the burden of his past actions were heavy on his shoulders. The guilt he felt over the fall of the gods and the realization of his own role in their betrayal were almost unbearable. He had hoped that retrieving the Crown would be a path to redemption, but instead, it had become a source of torment.

As they settled in for the night, Mira's mind raced with strategies and possible solutions. The Crown's true purpose remained a mystery, but its corrupting influence was becoming more apparent with each passing day. She knew that Kade's struggle was not just with the Crown but also with himself. The internal conflict he faced was as dangerous as any external threat, and she had to find a way to help him before it was too late.

The night was interrupted by distant sounds of movement. Kade's senses, honed by years of combat and survival, picked up on the subtle disturbances in the night. He tensed, his hand instinctively reaching for the sword at his side.

"Someone's coming," he whispered, his voice sharp with alertness.

Mira's eyes narrowed as she focused on the approaching sounds. "We need to move," she said, her voice steady. "Quickly."

The two of them gathered their belongings and prepared to leave. The sense of urgency was palpable, their earlier conversation forgotten in the face of imminent danger. As they moved through the forest, the shadows seemed to close in around them, the darkness of the night mirroring the uncertainty that hung over their journey.

Their escape led them through a series of winding paths and hidden trails, each step taking them farther from the safety of their temporary refuge. Mira led the way, her mage's instincts guiding them through the maze of trees and underbrush. Kade followed closely, his thoughts consumed by the looming threats and the weight of the Crown. The path ahead was fraught with peril, but the immediate danger of pursuit drove them forward.

As dawn approached, the forest began to lighten, and the first rays of sunlight pierced through the dense canopy. Kade and Mira emerged from the forest into a clearing, their breath coming in heavy gasps. The pursuit had slowed, but the danger was far from over. The time they had bought with their flight was fleeting, and they needed to find a way to continue their quest while avoiding capture.

"We can't keep running forever," Mira said, her voice tinged with frustration. "We need to find allies or a way to neutralize the Crown's influence."

Kade nodded, his expression grim. "I know. But where do we start? The world is a vast and dangerous place, and our enemies are many."

Mira's gaze was thoughtful as she considered their options. "There might be places or people who can help us understand the Crown's true nature. We need to find a way to break its hold over you and figure out how to use it—or destroy it—before it's too late."

Their discussion was interrupted by the sound of approaching footsteps. Kade and Mira quickly took cover, their eyes scanning the area for any sign of danger. A group of riders emerged from the treeline, their appearance a mix of relief and apprehension. The riders were clad in the colors of a faction Kade recognized—one that had been an ally in the past but had recently turned against him.

Kade tensed, ready to defend himself and Mira if necessary. The riders stopped at a safe distance, their leader—a tall, stern figure with a scarred face—dismounted and approached cautiously.

"Kade," the leader said, his voice carrying a mix of authority and curiosity, "we've been searching for you."

Kade's eyes narrowed. "What do you want? Why have you come after us?"

The leader's gaze was steady as he spoke. "We've heard rumors about the Crown and the darkness it brings. We believe you may hold the key to stopping it, but we need to understand more about its true nature."

Mira exchanged a glance with Kade, her expression unreadable. The offer of assistance was tempting, but the risks were considerable. Trusting these new allies could be a gamble, but their knowledge and resources might be the very thing they needed.

Kade took a deep breath, the weight of the Crown heavy on his mind. "Very well," he said finally, "we'll discuss our options. But know this: if you betray us, we will not hesitate to defend ourselves."

The leader nodded, a flicker of understanding in his eyes. "Agreed. We need to find a way to stop the impending darkness, and it seems we share a common goal."

As Kade and Mira joined the riders, the journey ahead remained fraught with uncertainty. The Crown's true purpose was still shrouded in mystery, and the path to salvation was unclear. The fractures within their group and the threats from all sides made their mission more perilous than ever. Yet, with every step they took, they moved closer to uncovering the truth and facing the challenges that lay ahead.

The flight from Blackstone Keep was far from over, and the pursuit would only grow more intense. As they rode through the changing landscape, the weight of the Crown and the shadows of their past actions loomed over them, driving them forward into the unknown.

Chapter 10: The Rise of the Fallen

The Crown of the Fallen, now an oppressive weight in Kade's hands, pulsed with a dark energy that seemed to warp reality itself. Its intricate patterns, once just symbols of forgotten power, now writhed with a malevolent life. Kade could feel its influence gnawing at his sanity, but it was the visions that truly unsettled him.

In the dim light of the forest clearing where Kade and Mira had taken refuge, shadows danced as if alive. The Crown lay between them, its power tangible in the oppressive air. Mira's eyes were dark with concern as she watched Kade pace restlessly, each step heavy with the burden of impending doom.

"These visions are growing worse," Mira said, her voice trembling slightly. She was visibly pale, her usual confidence overshadowed by the fear of what lay ahead. "You need to focus. We can't let this thing control you."

Kade's response was a mere grunt, his gaze fixed on the Crown. He was losing himself to the visions, his mind slipping into dark recesses where ancient evils stirred. In the fragmented reality of his vision, a figure emerged—dark and immense, bound in chains of shadow and blood. This entity, though not fully visible, exuded an aura of pure dread.

The figure's voice echoed in Kade's mind, a rasping whisper that promised both power and destruction. "Kade... You are the key to my release. The Crown will unlock the path, but only if you relinquish your hold on the world."

Shaking off the voice, Kade forced himself back to reality. He looked at Mira, who was now kneeling beside the Crown, trying to understand its arcane power. Her fingers brushed against its surface, and she recoiled immediately. The sensation was like touching a live wire, sending a shiver through her body.

"We need to find out what this really does," Mira said, her eyes meeting Kade's with a newfound determination. "There must be a way to understand its true purpose without letting it consume us."

Kade nodded, but his mind was elsewhere. He was haunted by the image of Lyra, his lost daughter, and the realization that she was the vessel for the ancient evil. The visions were relentless, showing him snippets of a future where the world was engulfed in chaos and darkness, ruled by the entity that the gods had once imprisoned.

"I have to see her again," Kade said abruptly, his voice strained. "I need to find Lyra before it's too late."

Mira's eyes widened with realization. "Lyra... She's still alive? And she's connected to this?"

"Yes," Kade replied, his tone grim. "She's the key to the entity's release. I have to find her before the Crown does its work."

With that, Kade and Mira packed their things quickly, the urgency of their mission outweighing their need for rest. The forest around them seemed to close in, the trees whispering secrets of forgotten times and impending doom.

Their journey took them back through the war-torn land, where the remnants of battles and the chaos of the crumbling empire painted a bleak picture. The once-thriving cities were now mere shadows of their former selves, and the roads were filled with the desperate and the dangerous.

They reached the outskirts of the city of Rethnor, where rumors of Lyra's whereabouts had surfaced. Kade's heart pounded with a mix of hope and fear as they approached the city's edge. The place was a labyrinth of alleyways and ruins, a perfect hideout for someone desperate to remain unseen.

The search through the city was exhausting. They questioned informants and braved through shady taverns, all the while trying to piece together the scattered hints about Lyra's location. Each step seemed to lead them deeper into a mire of uncertainty, and Kade could feel the Crown's dark influence growing stronger.

One night, as they rested in a dilapidated inn, Mira examined an old map she had acquired. Her brow furrowed in concentration as she traced a route with her finger. "There's an old shrine outside the city. It might be a place where Lyra could be hiding."

Kade's heart leaped. The shrine was mentioned in ancient texts he had studied long ago. It was said to be a place of old magic, once used by the gods themselves. "We need to go there," he said firmly. "It's our best lead."

As dawn broke, they set out towards the shrine, their path fraught with danger. The land around the shrine was rugged and unwelcoming, marked by jagged rocks and twisted vegetation. The shrine itself was a crumbling edifice, half-buried under vines and earth, its grandeur long forgotten.

Kade and Mira entered cautiously, their steps echoing in the hollow space. Inside, the shrine's interior was a maze of faded murals and broken statues, each depicting scenes of divine power and ancient rituals. As they ventured deeper, the air grew colder, and the atmosphere thickened with an eerie stillness.

At the heart of the shrine, they discovered a hidden chamber. The entrance was concealed by a sliding stone, which Kade and Mira managed to move with great effort. Inside, the chamber was illuminated by a faint, otherworldly glow. On a pedestal in the center of the room rested a figure wrapped in a dark cloak—Lyra.

Kade's breath caught in his throat. She was older now, her features sharp and haunted. As he approached, her eyes, once bright with childhood innocence, now held a depth of sorrow and power.

"Lyra..." Kade whispered, his voice breaking. He reached out to her, but she stepped back, her expression conflicted.

"Kade," Lyra said softly, her voice a mixture of pain and resignation. "I knew you would come, but it's too late. The Crown has awakened what was meant to be kept hidden."

Mira's eyes widened. "What do you mean? What is this place?"

Lyra looked at them both with a heavy heart. "This shrine is a place of binding, meant to hold the evil that the gods could not destroy. But the Crown... it is unlocking what was sealed away. I am the vessel, and now the ancient evil is stirring."

Kade's heart sank as the weight of the truth crashed down upon him. His own bloodline was intertwined with the ancient evil. The realization of what he had to do gnawed at him, filling him with dread.

"We have to stop this," Mira said urgently. "If the Crown has awakened the evil, we need to find a way to contain it before it's too late."

Lyra's eyes filled with tears. "It's not just the Crown. It's me. I am the key to the entity's release. To save the world, you will have to sacrifice me."

Kade's hands clenched into fists. "No... there must be another way. There has to be."

Lyra shook her head. "There isn't. The entity's power is too great. Only by giving up what it needs can we hope to contain it once more."

The words hung heavy in the air, a grim echo of the impossible choice that lay ahead. Kade's mind raced with thoughts of the world that could be lost, the daughter he had found but was destined to lose again.

Mira placed a comforting hand on Kade's shoulder. "We need to act quickly. The entity is stirring, and time is running out."

Kade nodded, his resolve hardening. "We'll find a way to stop this. We must."

The shrine seemed to close in around them as they prepared for the final confrontation. The fate of the world rested on their shoulders, and the path ahead was fraught with peril and sacrifice. The Crown's power, the awakening evil, and the destiny of Lyra were now intertwined in a tangled web of ancient prophecy and dark magic.

Kade staggered through the night-shrouded forest, the Crown of the Fallen clutched tightly in his gloved hands. The relic's cold weight seemed to drag at his very soul, its dark aura pulsing with an energy that gnawed at his sanity. The forest was silent except for the distant rustling of leaves, a far cry from the clamor of the battle they had just narrowly escaped.

Behind him, Mira's hurried footsteps were a constant reminder of their perilous situation. Her face, illuminated by the dim light of the moon, was etched with worry and determination. She had stayed with him despite the fractures in their alliance, a testament to her unwavering commitment.

"Do you feel it too?" Mira's voice cut through the silence, tinged with an edge of desperation. "The power within the Crown—it's growing stronger."

Kade nodded, though he did not trust his own words. "Yes. It's like it's feeding off my fear and anger. I can hardly think straight."

They reached a small clearing, where Kade motioned for them to stop. The ancient trees, twisted and gnarled, seemed to lean in, as if eager to hear the decisions of the forsaken warrior. Kade's mind was a storm of conflicting thoughts and emotions, all converging on the single, horrifying truth: Lyra was the vessel for the ancient evil, and he had to make a choice that would tear his heart in two.

Lyra—his daughter—whom he had thought lost to the ravages of time and conflict, had become something unimaginable. The visions he had experienced since touching the Crown had been harrowing. He had seen glimpses of her, surrounded by dark energies, a living conduit for the ancient evil that had once been imprisoned by the gods.

Mira approached him, her eyes fixed on the Crown. "Kade, we need to find a way to save her. There must be another option."

Her words, though filled with hope, were no more than a balm for Kade's deepening despair. He wanted to believe there was another way, but the revelations had been unrelenting. The ancient texts and cryptic messages from the oracle had left no room for doubt—the only way to prevent the ancient evil from consuming the world was to destroy the vessel, his own flesh and blood.

As if reading his thoughts, Mira continued, her voice softer now. "You're not alone in this. We'll figure something out. There's always a way."

But Kade could not shake the image of Lyra from his mind. He remembered her as a child, full of laughter and light, a beacon in the darkness of his life. Now, she was the darkness itself. The weight of his impending decision was almost too much to bear.

They pressed on, the forest giving way to rocky terrain. As they climbed the craggy slopes, the stars above seemed to mock their desperate quest. Kade's thoughts turned inward, struggling with the unbearable choice he had to make. Each step felt like a march toward doom, a grim pilgrimage that would end in a sacrifice beyond comprehension.

Eventually, they reached a secluded cave high in the mountains, hidden from prying eyes. The cave was a sanctuary of sorts, its cold, damp interior offering a brief respite from their relentless journey. Kade and Mira entered, the darkness inside echoing their troubled minds.

Mira set up a small campfire, its flickering light casting eerie shadows on the cave walls. She glanced at Kade, concern evident in her eyes. "We need to rest and regroup. The Crown's power is affecting you more than it should. We can't afford to be reckless."

Kade nodded, though he could not shake the heavy burden that pressed on his shoulders. As Mira prepared a simple meal, Kade stared at the Crown, which lay on a flat rock, its malevolent presence filling the small space. He had hoped the darkness within would dissipate, but instead, it seemed to grow stronger with every passing moment.

Hours passed in strained silence. Mira, though clearly exhausted, remained vigilant. Kade, meanwhile, wrestled with his thoughts, haunted by dreams of his daughter's face twisted in agony. The images were relentless, each one a dagger to his heart, a reminder of the cruel fate that awaited him.

Finally, Mira broke the silence, her voice barely above a whisper. "Kade, what's the plan? We can't stay here forever."

He looked at her, his expression one of deep sorrow. "There's no plan, Mira. The Crown holds the key to the ancient evil's release, and Lyra is its vessel. I have to confront her and make the choice that will save—or doom—us all."

Mira's eyes widened in shock. "You mean to say... you have to kill her?"

Kade's silence was answer enough. The weight of the words seemed to hang in the air like a dense fog, suffocating any hope they might have had. Mira's face fell, and she turned away, struggling to come to terms with the enormity of their situation.

A sudden noise broke the quiet—a rustling at the entrance of the cave. Kade and Mira tensed, their senses on high alert. Kade grabbed his sword, the steel cold and comforting in his hand. Mira prepared a spell, her fingers crackling with latent magic.

The source of the noise emerged—a figure cloaked in shadow, its face obscured. As it stepped into the firelight, Kade recognized the figure. It was Sorin, their erstwhile companion who had disappeared during the siege at Blackstone Keep.

Sorin's face was haggard, his eyes reflecting a weariness that spoke of untold struggles. "Kade, Mira. I've been searching for you."

Kade's grip on his sword tightened. "Sorin? Why have you returned?"

Sorin's gaze flicked to the Crown, his expression unreadable. "I had to see it for myself. I had to understand the truth. I know what you're facing, Kade. And I've come to offer my help."

Mira's skepticism was palpable. "And why should we trust you now? After everything that happened?"

Sorin's shoulders slumped. "Because I've learned something that might change everything. The prophecy—the one that speaks of the ancient evil—it's not just about the Crown. It's about a choice that can alter the course of history."

Kade and Mira exchanged wary glances. "What do you mean?" Kade asked, his voice rough.

Sorin stepped closer, lowering his voice. "There is another way. A hidden power within the Crown, a way to bind the ancient evil without sacrificing Lyra. But it requires a ritual, one that has been lost to time. I've found fragments of the old texts. With them, we might be able to perform the ritual and contain the evil."

The words were a sliver of hope amidst their dire situation. Kade's heart pounded with a mix of relief and skepticism. "Where are these texts?"

Sorin reached into his cloak and produced a tattered scroll. "I found this among the ruins. It's incomplete, but it might be enough. We need to perform the ritual at the old temple—one of the last remaining sites of the gods' influence."

Kade took the scroll, feeling the rough texture of the ancient parchment beneath his fingers. The promise of an alternative method to save his daughter was a beacon of hope, but it also raised a new set of uncertainties. Could they trust Sorin's knowledge? Was there truly a chance to avoid the horrifying choice before him?

Mira looked at Kade, her eyes filled with a mixture of hope and apprehension. "We have to try, Kade. It's the only chance we have."

Kade nodded, a determined resolve settling over him. "Then we leave at first light. We have to reach the temple and see if this ritual can truly bind the ancient evil. If there's even a chance to save Lyra, we must take it."

As they settled into a restless sleep, the flickering flames of the campfire cast dancing shadows on the cave walls, mirroring the tumultuous emotions that churned within each of them. The dawn of a new day would bring them closer to their destiny, but the path ahead was fraught with uncertainty and danger.

Kade's dreams were haunted by visions of his daughter, twisted and tormented by the dark forces that sought to consume her. He knew that whatever awaited them at the old temple, it would be a final, desperate gamble to redeem his past and secure a future for his daughter and the world. The weight of his decision loomed larger than ever, a shadow over his every step.

The rising sun heralded a new chapter in their journey, one that would test their resolve, their unity, and their very souls. As Kade and his companions prepared for the trials ahead, they knew that the choices made in the coming days would shape the fate of the world—and determine whether the ancient evil would rise or be bound once more.

Their journey to the old temple was more than just a quest; it was a crucible that would reveal the true strength of their bonds and the depth of their sacrifices. The echoes of the gods' fall resonated through their every step, and the promise of redemption hung in the balance, a fragile thread that might unravel with the slightest misstep.

As the cave receded into the distance, Kade and his companions forged ahead, each step a testament to their determination and hope. The path was fraught with danger, but they pressed on, driven by the knowledge that their choices would echo through the ages.

Chapter 11: The Battle for the World

The skies above the ancient ruins of Elaria were churning with a dark, tumultuous energy. Lightning crackled through the dark clouds, illuminating the twisted silhouettes of the once-great temples that now stood as broken sentinels of a forgotten age. The air was thick with the scent of burning wood and the acrid tang of magic gone awry. Kade stood at the forefront of the battlefield, his gaze fixed on the shadows gathering in the distance. The Crown of the Fallen, now a blighted relic, pulsed with a malevolent glow on his brow, its power seeping into him like poison.

The remnants of his party, now fewer and far less hopeful than when they first set out, had gathered around him. Mira, her robes tattered and her face etched with weariness, stood resolutely beside him. Her once-brilliant eyes were now shadowed with a deep sorrow. Tyra, battle-worn but determined, was checking her weapons with grim efficiency. The echoes of their past battles and the scars they carried were a testament to their journey. Sorin, the stoic mercenary who had once been an antagonist, was now an ally. His grizzled face showed both fatigue and resolve. Together, they faced the encroaching darkness with a courage born of shared suffering.

The battlefield stretched out before them, a chaotic expanse of clashing forces. The armies of the warring factions, drawn by the promise of power or the drive to protect their realms, had converged on Elaria. They clashed in a cacophony of steel and sorcery, a roiling tempest of conflict that threatened to tear the world apart. Amidst this maelstrom, Kade's eyes were drawn to the center of the chaos, where the ancient evil was beginning to manifest. It was a shadowy form, nebulous and shifting, as if it were both everywhere and nowhere, a void in the fabric of reality.

Kade's grip tightened around the hilt of his blade, its once-pure silver now tarnished by the corrupting influence of the Crown. The weapon had been a symbol of his faith, a conduit of divine power. Now, it felt like a weight dragging him down, a reminder of his failures and the darkness he had unwittingly unleashed. Every strike he made with it seemed to echo with the wrath of the ancient evil, his movements more desperate than deliberate.

The forces of darkness, summoned by the Crown's corrupting aura, began to take form. Nightmarish creatures emerged from the shadows, their bodies twisted and malformed, driven by an insatiable hunger for destruction. These were not mere beasts but corrupted reflections of once-noble entities, twisted by the malevolent force that had been unleashed.

Mira's incantations cut through the din of battle, her magic a desperate shield against the encroaching darkness. She chanted spells with a fierce intensity, her hands weaving complex patterns in the air as she summoned barriers of light to protect their position. Each spell she cast was a battle against the tide of corruption that sought to engulf them all. Yet, even her formidable power seemed strained by the overwhelming presence of the ancient evil.

Tyra, agile and swift, darted through the battlefield with a precision that belied her youth. Her nimble movements allowed her to strike at the heart of the enemy forces, her daggers flashing with deadly accuracy. She fought with a fervor that spoke of her desire to prove herself, to show that despite her youth and inexperience, she could stand against the forces of darkness. Each of her strikes was a testament to her resolve, each step a defiance of the fate that had brought them to this dire moment.

Sorin, ever the pragmatist, directed the remnants of their forces with a cold efficiency. His battle-hardened experience made him an invaluable leader on the battlefield. He moved with a purpose, coordinating attacks and rallying their allies in a desperate bid to stem the tide of darkness. His eyes, though weary, were sharp, and his commands were carried out with a precision that was both awe-inspiring and terrifying.

Kade's mind was a tempest of conflicting emotions. He knew that this battle was not merely a fight for survival but a fight for the very soul of the world. The ancient evil that had been bound by the gods was now free, and its presence was a blight upon the land. He could feel its influence gnawing at the edges of his consciousness, a relentless whisper promising despair and ruin. Yet, amidst the chaos, Kade found a glimmer of hope. The world still fought, still clung to the fragile hope of survival.

As the battle raged, Kade could see that the forces of the ancient evil were not merely attacking but were attempting to draw power from the very ground they fought on. The earth itself seemed to writhe and convulse as if it were in pain. The energy of the Crown was drawing upon the land, corrupting it and feeding the ancient evil's power. Kade realized that to defeat this foe, they would need to sever its connection to the land and to the Crown.

Amidst the din of battle, Kade's thoughts were drawn to his daughter, Lyra. The revelation of her being the vessel for the ancient evil had torn his heart in ways he could barely comprehend. His love for her and his duty to save the world were at odds, creating an unbearable tension within him. Every glance he took toward the shadowed figure at the heart of the battlefield was a reminder of the choice he had to make.

The ancient evil began to coalesce into a more tangible form, a dark entity of immense power and malice. Its presence seemed to suck the light and hope from the air, leaving only a void in its wake. The entity moved with a deliberate grace, a predatory elegance that suggested an intelligence far beyond mortal comprehension. It was both a terror and a tragedy, a reminder of the gods' fall and the catastrophic consequences of their betrayal.

Kade, driven by a grim determination, fought his way toward the heart of the battlefield, where the ancient evil was beginning to materialize fully. His movements were fierce, a testament to his will to protect what remained of the world. The air crackled with the tension of impending doom, the very fabric of reality seeming to fray as the ancient evil's power grew.

Mira, sensing the gravity of the situation, unleashed a powerful spell that created a temporary barrier around Kade. Her eyes were filled with an intensity that spoke of her desperation and her own inner struggle. She had seen the prophecy, understood the implications of their actions, and now fought with a fierce resolve to ensure that their efforts were not in vain.

Tyra, ever the vigilant warrior, fought her way to Kade's side, her movements a blur of speed and precision. She glanced at him with a mix of determination and concern, understanding the weight of the choices he faced. Her support, though unspoken, was a crucial element in their fight against the encroaching darkness.

Sorin's voice cut through the chaos, directing their forces with a steady hand. His experience and leadership were a beacon amidst the turmoil, guiding their allies and coordinating their efforts. He fought with a grim resolve, knowing that the fate of the world hinged on their actions.

As Kade approached the heart of the battlefield, the ancient evil's presence became overwhelming. It was a dark vortex of energy, a swirling maelstrom of corruption that seemed to pulse with a rhythm of its own. The entity's eyes, if they could be called that, were empty voids, reflecting the darkness of the abyss from which it had emerged.

Kade steeled himself, pushing through the oppressive force of the ancient evil. The Crown of the Fallen throbbed with a dark energy, its power a constant reminder of the evil it had unleashed. Kade knew that he had to reach the entity's core, to sever its connection to the world and to the Crown.

The battle around him was a maelstrom of chaos, the forces of darkness pressing in from all sides. Kade fought with a desperation born of necessity, each swing of his blade a testament to his resolve. The air was filled with the clash of steel, the roar of spells, and the cries of the wounded. Every step he took was a step closer to the heart of the darkness, a step closer to the confrontation that would determine the fate of the world.

In the midst of the chaos, Kade could see his allies fighting with a fierce determination. Mira's spells illuminated the battlefield with bursts of light, cutting through the darkness and providing brief moments of clarity. Tyra's agility and precision made her a deadly force against the enemies, her movements a dance of destruction. Sorin's leadership and coordination were a crucial element in their defense, guiding their forces and ensuring their survival.

As Kade reached the core of the ancient evil, he faced the entity's true form. It was a dark, swirling vortex of malevolent energy, an embodiment of the corruption and chaos that had been unleashed. The entity's presence was overwhelming, a suffocating force that seemed to consume everything in its vicinity.

Kade's mind was a whirlwind of thoughts and emotions. He knew that this battle was not just a physical confrontation but a test of his will and resolve. The choices he had made, the sacrifices he had endured, and the love he had for his daughter all weighed heavily on him. He could feel the Crown's influence growing stronger, its power a constant reminder of the darkness he was fighting against.

The final confrontation was a brutal and relentless struggle, a clash of wills and power that pushed Kade to his limits. The entity's attacks were devastating, each blow a reminder of the corruption and chaos it represented. Yet, amidst the darkness, Kade fought with a determination that bordered on desperation. He knew that the fate of the world hinged on his ability to overcome the ancient evil and to free his daughter from its grasp.

As the battle raged on, Kade's thoughts turned to the prophecy, to the future that lay beyond this confrontation. He knew that the world would not be the same, that the cost of their victory would be great. Yet, amidst the chaos, he clung to the hope that their efforts would not be in vain, that the world could be salvaged from the brink of destruction.

The final moments of the battle were a blur of chaos and power. Kade's strikes were fueled by a mixture of anger, hope, and desperation. The entity's form began to fracture, its presence destabilizing as Kade's efforts bore fruit. The Crown of the Fallen, once a symbol of darkness, now seemed to resonate with a flicker of light, a sign that the ancient evil's grip on the world was weakening.

With a final, desperate surge of power, Kade unleashed a devastating attack, channeling every ounce of his strength and resolve into a single, decisive blow. The ancient evil's form shattered, its presence disintegrating into a cascade of dark energy. The darkness that had once threatened to consume the world began to recede, its power waning as the entity was vanquished.

The battlefield fell into a stunned silence, the chaos and destruction giving way to a fragile peace. The forces of darkness had been defeated, and the world had been spared from the brink of annihilation. Yet, the cost of victory was evident in the scars and losses that marked the aftermath.

Kade stood amidst the ruins, his breath coming in ragged gasps. The Crown of the Fallen lay on the ground before him, its dark energy now dormant. The weight of the battle's toll was evident in his weary eyes and battered form. He knew that the world would not be the same, that the aftermath of this conflict would require healing and rebuilding.

As the survivors of the battle gathered around him, Kade felt a mixture of relief and sorrow. The fight was over, but the scars of the battle would remain. The world had been spared from the ancient evil, but the cost of their victory was a heavy burden to bear. Kade's gaze fell upon his allies, each of them bearing the marks of their struggle. Their faces were a mix of exhaustion and determination, a reflection of the battle they had fought and the future they now faced.

Mira, her face drawn and tired, approached Kade with a look of solemn gratitude. Her magic had been a crucial element in their victory, and her sacrifices were evident in the exhaustion that marked her every movement. Tyra, her youthful face now etched with the weight of the battle, nodded at Kade with a mixture of respect and relief. Sorin, ever the pragmatist, surveyed the battlefield with a critical eye, his leadership having been instrumental in their success.

The ancient evil had been defeated, but the world was left to pick up the pieces. The prophecy had been fulfilled, and the future remained uncertain. Kade knew that their journey was not over, that the road to redemption and healing would be long and arduous. Yet, amidst the uncertainty, he clung to the hope that their efforts had made a difference, that the world could be rebuilt and that the lessons learned from their struggle would guide them toward a brighter future.

As the sun began to rise over the ruined landscape, casting a hopeful light upon the battered world, Kade took a deep breath and faced the uncertain future with a renewed sense of purpose. The battle had been won, but the journey ahead was one of healing and rebuilding. The world had been spared from the brink of destruction, and now it was up to those who had fought to ensure that the scars of the past would not define the future.

The sun's rays filtered through the remnants of the ancient city, casting a warm and hopeful light over the broken landscape. The once-great temples and structures of Elaria now stood as silent witnesses to the battle that had taken place. The ruins, though scarred and battered, held a promise of renewal and rebirth.

Kade stood amidst the remnants of the battlefield, the weight of his armor and the Crown of the Fallen a constant reminder of the cost of their victory. The Crown, now stripped of its dark power, lay beside him, its once-malevolent energy reduced to a mere relic of the past. Kade's gaze was drawn to the horizon, where the first light of dawn was breaking through the clouds. The world was waking from the darkness, and with it came a sense of cautious hope.

Mira, Tyra, and Sorin gathered around Kade, their faces reflecting a mixture of exhaustion and relief. The battle had taken its toll on them, but their resolve remained unbroken. The once-clear lines of battle had blurred into a shared experience of struggle and triumph, a bond forged in the crucible of conflict.

Mira's magic had been instrumental in their victory, her spells a beacon of light amidst the darkness. She surveyed the battlefield with a tired but hopeful expression, her eyes reflecting the promise of a new beginning. Tyra, her youthful energy now tempered by the reality of their ordeal, looked to the horizon with a determined gaze. Her role in the battle had been pivotal, her bravery and skill a testament to her growth and resolve. Sorin, ever the pragmatist, was already assessing the damage and beginning to formulate plans for rebuilding. His leadership and experience would be crucial in the efforts to restore order and stability.

As the survivors began to emerge from the shadows, the true scale of the aftermath became apparent. The once-great city of Elaria was in ruins, its grandeur reduced to broken stone and twisted metal. Yet, amidst the destruction, there were signs of life and hope. The people who had once called Elaria home were beginning to gather, their faces reflecting a mixture of grief and determination.

Kade's heart ached as he looked upon the survivors. They were the ones who would bear the scars of the battle, the ones who would rebuild and carry forward the lessons learned from their struggle. He knew that their journey was far from over, that the path to recovery and renewal would be long and fraught with challenges.

In the days that followed, Kade and his allies worked tirelessly to assist in the rebuilding efforts. The task was daunting, but there was a sense of unity and purpose that guided their efforts. The survivors, though weary, were determined to restore their world and honor the sacrifices made during the battle.

Mira's magic became a symbol of hope and renewal. Her spells were used to heal the land and aid in the reconstruction of the city. The once-dying magic of Elaria began to awaken, its ancient power slowly being restored. Mira's efforts were a testament to her resilience and her commitment to the future.

Tyra's bravery and skill were instrumental in organizing the survivors and coordinating the rebuilding efforts. Her youthful energy and determination inspired those around her, and her leadership became a beacon of hope amidst the challenges they faced. Her role in the battle had transformed her from a mere warrior into a symbol of courage and resilience.

Sorin's experience and pragmatism guided the restoration efforts, his strategic mind essential in organizing the reconstruction and ensuring that the city was rebuilt with a vision for the future. His leadership and expertise were crucial in navigating the complexities of the rebuilding process, and his efforts helped to lay the foundation for a renewed Elaria.

As the city began to take shape once more, Kade found solace in the small victories and the gradual return of hope. The world was healing, its wounds slowly mending. The darkness that had threatened to consume everything had been vanquished, and a new dawn was breaking.

Kade's thoughts often turned to his daughter, Lyra. The revelation of her being the vessel for the ancient evil had been a devastating blow, but he found a measure of peace in knowing that she was free from the darkness that had once held her captive. His love for her and his desire to protect her had been a driving force throughout the battle, and now, he hoped that she could find her own path to healing and redemption.

The journey to restore Elaria and the world was far from complete, but the efforts of Kade and his allies were a testament to their resolve and their hope for a brighter future. The scars of the past were still visible, but they were accompanied by a sense of renewal and possibility. The world had faced its darkest hour and emerged stronger for it.

As Kade stood amidst the rebuilding city, he took a deep breath and embraced the new dawn. The battle was over, and the future lay ahead, filled with both challenges and opportunities. The world had been saved, and with it came the chance to build a future that honored the sacrifices made and the lessons learned.

The path forward would be long and difficult, but Kade and his allies were ready to face it with hope and determination. The world had been given a second chance, and it was up to them to ensure that it was a chance that would be seized and cherished.

With the first light of dawn casting its warm glow over the city, Kade looked to the horizon and embraced the promise of a new beginning. The battle for the world had been won, and now, the true challenge lay in the journey of rebuilding and renewal. The world was waking from its darkness, and with it came the hope of a brighter and more hopeful future.

Chapter 12: The Shattered Crown

The world had grown silent in the wake of the battle's end. The once-grand empire of Rethnor, now a shadow of its former self, lay in ruins, its cities devastated by the conflict that had raged across the land. The remnants of the ancient world were scattered across the broken landscape, a testament to the cost of their victory.

Kade stood amidst the wreckage, the weight of his sacrifice heavy upon his shoulders. The land was scarred, and the sky was a dismal grey, as if mourning the destruction that had befallen it. The ancient ruins of Rethnor, once a symbol of power and divinity, now lay in tatters. The fallen structures, shattered statues, and the remnants of once-mighty temples were all that remained of a once-glorious civilization.

Mira, her face etched with fatigue and sorrow, walked beside Kade. The battle had taken a toll on her, but her resolve remained unshaken. Her eyes were drawn to the broken remains of the Silent Temple, a place that had once held great significance for Kade and his fallen order. The temple was now a somber monument to the gods' silence, a reminder of the power they had lost and the darkness that had almost consumed the world.

Tyra and Sorin joined them, their expressions reflecting a mixture of exhaustion and reflection. Tyra, once a hopeful thief with dreams of seeing the gods, now carried the burden of witnessing their downfall and the true cost of the Crown. Sorin, ever the pragmatist, surveyed the damage with a critical eye, his mind already turning to the logistics of rebuilding.

The silence that followed the battle was a stark contrast to the chaos and clamor of the conflict. It was a heavy, oppressive silence that spoke of loss and the weight of what had transpired. The survivors, those who had lived through the final confrontation, moved among the ruins with a sense of weary determination. They were the ones who would rebuild, who would face the aftermath of the battle and the consequences of their choices.

Mira's gaze fell upon the shattered remains of the Crown of the Fallen, which lay abandoned in the midst of the ruins. The Crown, once a symbol of hope and power, was now a broken relic, its dark energy dispersed. The final confrontation had revealed the true nature of the Crown—it was not a tool for salvation, but a key to unlocking the ancient evil that had once been bound by the gods. The truth had come at a terrible price, and Kade's sacrifice had been the only way to prevent the world from falling into eternal darkness.

The survivors gathered around the remnants of the Crown, their expressions a mixture of sadness and relief. The Crown's power had been vanquished, but the cost of their victory had left a profound impact on all of them. The world was saved, but the empire lay in ruins, and the scars of the battle were etched into the land and its people.

Mira's voice broke the silence. "We have achieved what we set out to do, but at what cost? The world is broken, and the gods are still silent. What do we do now?"

Kade's gaze was distant, his thoughts consumed by the aftermath of his actions. "We rebuild," he said quietly. "We honor the sacrifices made and strive to create a future from the ashes of the past."

Tyra looked up at Kade, her eyes reflecting a mix of admiration and sorrow. "You gave everything to save us," she said. "But what will become of us now?"

Sorin, ever the realist, spoke up. "The world may be saved, but it is far from healed. We have much work to do if we are to rebuild and ensure that the darkness does not return."

As they surveyed the ruins, the enormity of their task became clear. The battle had been won, but the world was left to pick up the pieces. The remnants of the empire, once a symbol of divine power, were now a stark reminder of the cost of their struggle. The gods' silence remained a haunting question, and the future was uncertain.

Kade's thoughts turned to his daughter, Lyra. The revelation that she was the vessel for the ancient evil had been a devastating blow, and her loss was a heavy burden he would carry for the rest of his life. The choice he had been forced to make—sacrificing his own flesh and blood to save the world—had left him hollow and grief-stricken. He could only hope that her sacrifice would bring about a new beginning for the world, even if it meant living with the weight of his actions.

Mira approached Kade, her hand resting gently on his shoulder. "We cannot change the past," she said softly. "But we can shape the future. Let us not forget the lessons learned and the sacrifices made. We must ensure that the world does not fall into darkness again."

Kade nodded, his gaze still fixed on the broken remains of the Crown. "You are right. We have a chance to make things right, to build a future that honors those who came before us."

As the survivors began to gather the remnants of the Crown and prepare for the task of rebuilding, a new sense of purpose emerged. The battle may have been won, but the journey to restore the world was just beginning. The future was uncertain, but there was a glimmer of hope that, despite the devastation, the world could rise from the ashes and forge a new path forward.

The ancient empire of Rethnor was a shattered kingdom, but its people were resilient. They would rebuild, not only the physical structures but also the spirit of their civilization. The gods had been silent, but the echoes of their once-great power could still be felt in the land. It was up to the survivors to honor their legacy and ensure that their sacrifices had not been in vain.

Kade, Mira, Tyra, and Sorin stood together amid the ruins, a symbol of their unity and determination. The world had been saved from the brink of destruction, and now it was up to them to ensure that it was a world worth saving. The shattered Crown of the Fallen lay among the ruins, a reminder of the cost of their victory and the promise of a new beginning.

As the survivors began to make plans for the future, Kade looked to the horizon with a sense of cautious optimism. The path ahead was fraught with challenges, but it was a path they would walk together. The world had been given a second chance, and it was up to them to seize that chance and build a future from the remnants of the past.

The sun began to set over the ruined empire, casting long shadows over the desolate landscape. The darkness of the past was giving way to the promise of a new dawn, and with it came the hope that, despite the scars of the battle, the world could be renewed and rebuilt.

The dawn broke over the shattered remains of Rethnor like a hesitant whisper. The once-vibrant city now lay in ruins, a testament to the colossal struggle that had transpired. Smoke still curled in the cold morning air, mingling with the fog that clung to the remnants of fallen towers and broken walls. The battle for the world was over, but the cost had been immense.

Mira stood atop a hill overlooking the devastated capital, her gaze drifting over the wreckage. The crown of victory had come at the price of too many lives. She had seen Kade's sacrifice, felt the weight of it, and now she was left to grapple with the aftermath. Each step she took was heavy with the burden of their shared history, the price paid for a world that might yet heal.

Kade's final moments were still vivid in her mind. He had faced the darkness, not just the ancient evil, but the darkness within himself. The battle against the ancient evil had been fierce, but in the end, Kade had made a choice that would ripple through the ages. His sacrifice was not just a personal loss but a loss that echoed across the fabric of existence.

Mira moved slowly, as if the weight of her thoughts was anchoring her to the spot. The city below was scarred, and the people who had survived the siege and the battles were starting to emerge from their shelters. Among the survivors were those who had fought alongside Kade, those who had seen the true price of their victory. They were the ones who would rebuild, who would take up the mantle of forging a new future.

As she descended into the city, Mira encountered familiar faces—faces etched with the exhaustion of battle and the grief of loss. Sorin, the mercenary who had fought bravely despite his own reservations, was helping to organize the survivors, his usually gruff demeanor softened by the task at hand. Tyra, the young thief who had witnessed so much, was now a beacon of hope for the children who had been orphaned by the conflict.

The city's heart lay in ruins, but there was a spark of life amidst the desolation. People were starting to gather the pieces of their shattered lives, attempting to piece together what remained. Mira knew that rebuilding Rethnor would be no small feat. The city's spirit had been broken, but its people were resilient.

Mira entered the ruins of the Great Temple, once a place of worship now desecrated by the recent violence. She walked through the halls where the echoes of divine presence had been replaced by the heavy silence of loss. The temple had been Kade's sanctuary, and now it was a graveyard of dreams and ideals. It was here that the echoes of the past spoke the loudest, and Mira found herself drawn to the altar where Kade had once sought solace.

In the dim light of the early morning, Mira knelt before the altar, her hands resting on the cold stone. The relics of the gods had been lost, their power dissipated, but the memories of their once-glorious reign remained etched in the temple's walls. Kade's sacrifice had been a desperate attempt to undo the wrongs of a forgotten era, but in the end, it had only paved the way for a new dawn, one fraught with uncertainty and hope.

Mira's thoughts were interrupted by the sound of approaching footsteps. Sorin and Tyra arrived, their faces showing a mixture of determination and weariness. They had come to offer their support, and Mira welcomed their presence with a nod.

"We need to talk," Sorin said, his voice carrying the weight of their shared experience. "The survivors are starting to regroup, but we have to ensure that they have what they need to rebuild."

Tyra, her eyes reflecting the loss she had witnessed, added, "We have to find a way to honor Kade's sacrifice. He gave everything for this world, and we can't let it be in vain."

Mira agreed, her thoughts turning to the future. "We need to establish order, find a way to restore some semblance of normalcy. The gods may be gone, but we are not. We have to forge a new path, one that acknowledges the past but looks towards the future."

As the trio walked through the remains of the city, they encountered survivors who had begun to rebuild their lives. Among them were families trying to find each other, friends comforting one another, and leaders emerging from the chaos. The road to recovery would be long, but it was clear that the people of Rethnor were determined to move forward.

Mira and her companions worked tirelessly, organizing aid, providing shelter, and offering hope to those who needed it most. The city's heart was broken, but it was not beyond repair. The challenges ahead were daunting, but the resilience of the human spirit was a powerful force.

In the midst of their efforts, Mira discovered a small group of scholars who had survived the conflict. They were studying ancient texts and artifacts, trying to piece together the lost knowledge of the gods. Mira joined them, seeing the potential to rebuild the understanding of the divine and perhaps find a way to prevent future catastrophes.

As weeks turned into months, Rethnor began to show signs of recovery. The city's streets, once filled with the sounds of destruction, were now alive with the sounds of rebuilding. The survivors worked together, their efforts driven by a shared desire to honor those who had fallen and to create a new future.

In the quiet moments of reflection, Mira found herself pondering the nature of the gods and the true meaning of Kade's sacrifice. The Crown had not resurrected the gods, but it had paved the way for a new beginning. The world was not beyond redemption, and the future was still unwritten.

One evening, as Mira stood on the hill overlooking the city, she saw a group of children playing among the ruins. Their laughter was a poignant reminder that life continued despite the scars of the past. The legacy of Kade's sacrifice was not just in the restoration of a city, but in the hope that the next generation would grow up in a world where the mistakes of the past would not be repeated.

Mira's thoughts turned to a whispered prophecy she had heard in the temple. It had hinted at the possibility of a new beginning, a chance for the gods to return in some form. The prophecy had been vague, but it left her with a sense of anticipation. Perhaps the end was not as final as it seemed, and the world still held secrets waiting to be discovered.

As the sun set over Rethnor, Mira took a deep breath, feeling the cool evening air on her face. The journey had been arduous, and the cost had been high, but there was a glimmer of hope in the horizon. The shattered crown had marked the end of an era, but it had also set the stage for a new beginning.

With renewed determination, Mira turned her gaze towards the future, ready to face whatever challenges lay ahead. The legacy of Kade's sacrifice would guide her, and the promise of a new dawn would inspire her as she continued to shape the world that was emerging from the ashes of the old.

In the quiet stillness of the evening, Mira whispered a prayer for the fallen, for Kade, and for the world that had been forever changed. It was a prayer for healing, for hope, and for a future where the lessons of the past would lead to a brighter tomorrow.

The world had been shattered, but it was not beyond repair. The dawn had come, and with it, the promise of a new beginning.

Don't miss out!

Visit the website below and you can sign up to receive emails whenever Michael Ferguson publishes a new book. There's no charge and no obligation.

https://books2read.com/r/B-A-CKNW-KDJZE

BOOKS 2 READ

Connecting independent readers to independent writers.

Did you love *Shattered Crown*? Then you should read *Mindbreak*[1] by Michael Ferguson!

Dr. Elara Valen, a pioneering neuroscientist, achieves a groundbreaking feat with her Mindbreak technology: reviving coma patients and exploring their minds. When the government proposes a dangerous mission to delve into the psyche of notorious serial killer Cyrus Thorn, Elara and her team are thrust into a harrowing journey.

Entering Thorn's mind, the team is met with a surreal and nightmarish landscape that defies all expectations. Their initial exploration quickly turns into a struggle for survival as they

1. https://books2read.com/u/mYn69Y

2. https://books2read.com/u/mYn69Y

encounter grotesque visions and realize they are being hunted. Each step deeper into Thorn's twisted reality uncovers more horrifying traps and psychological torment, pushing them to the brink of insanity.

As the team navigates Thorn's labyrinthine mind, they discover that he is not merely a passive victim of Mindbreak but is actively controlling and manipulating their environment. The psychological and physical dangers intensify as Thorn's world fractures their perceptions, creating illusions and amplifying their deepest fears.

The situation grows more desperate as they confront Thorn's past crimes in a nightmarish cityscape and face the chilling reality of his influence. Elara and her trusted colleague Luka Nerin grapple with personal traumas that Thorn exploits, leading to a heart-wrenching climax where sacrifices are made to contain the killer's malevolent presence.

Upon returning to reality, the survivors are haunted by their experiences and discover unsettling evidence suggesting that Thorn's consciousness may not have been fully eradicated. As strange occurrences plague their lives, Luka suspects that Thorn's influence has found a new, more insidious way to spread.

In a final, high-stakes confrontation, Luka and the team make a desperate attempt to neutralize Thorn's lingering presence. Despite their efforts, they are left with a haunting uncertainty: some horrors, it seems, can never be fully contained. The story concludes with a chilling ambiguity, leaving readers questioning whether the nightmare is truly over—or if it has only just begun.